SHADOW SELF

RENEE LANDRUSS

Shadow Self
Copyright © 2024 by Renee Landruss

Library of Congress Control Number: 2024922219

ISBN
978-1-964982-77-9 (Paperback)
978-1-964982-78-6 (eBook)
978-1-964982-76-2 (Hardcover

For my husband, our three sons, and my special girls, who patiently watched our home and yard fill with spiritual paraphernalia and a labyrinth as I researched the supernatural world in order to write this book and the sequel.

My soul sisters, who encouraged me in each bizarre journey I have embarked on.

TABLE OF CONTENTS

"We are the ones we've been waiting for."

— The Elders, Oraibi, Arizona Hopi Nation

Psychic Journey

Light from the full moon divided the clouds and crept through slats of blinds that shielded the window, saturating the darkened living room with a soft glow, casting shadows across the walls.

Howls from a pack of wolves resonated from speakers and throughout the apartment. Justine slid open a tiny box, pulled out a match and scratched the red head along the side until it burst into a flare. She held the quivering flame over a candle. Beeswax softened, pooled on top and absorbed all scent of sulphur. Manicured fingers reached for a bale of sage and dangled it over the burn. Fragrance of herb flowed to her nostrils. Puffs of smoke billowed behind her arm waving the smudge. Light reflected from the mother-of-pearl as she butted the lit end into the abalone shell.

She pulled a blanket that draped the back of her chair, snapped the cover and let it flatten on the hardwood floor, slid it under her coffee table and tugged it into place. She pumped a feather pillow between her palms and positioned it onto the blanket, pulled an afghan from the sofa and sheathed it over the coffee table.

Stacks of meditation and shaman books sat next to her paraphernalia of essential oils, resin granules, smudges and powders. She squeezed a charcoal with tweezers and held it under the flame of the candle until it hissed with tiny sparks, settled the sizzling coal onto sand contained inside a miniature cauldron, flipped open a small wooden box, pulled out a pinch of powder and sprinkled it onto the burning coal. Fresh scent of cedar wafted through the air after the swirling smoke.

Excitement and fear swarmed inside her as she crawled into her grotto and rested her head on the pillow.

This time, I will not let fear stop me.

White translucent light followed a deep breath in. The orb floated to her toes, swelled and filled her to the crown. Beams escaped through the top of her head and wrapped itself around her like a heated blanket. She closed her eyes, drew a deep breath, released it at a slow pace, and entered a trance.

She shuffled down a long path, stumbling over protruding roots. Gusts of wind carried minute snowflakes across the sky. Rays of sunlight reflected off the falling flurry, creating an illusion of tiny tumbling crystals. Tall pine trees, hanging thick with lichen, spread out on either side of the trail.

Tiny green birds, sporting blue bellies under crimson feathers, scattered in the pale sky and descended toward her. A seductive song, full and throaty, filled the forest as the fowls settled on nearby branches. The smallest bird flew toward a long strand of lichen swaying in the wind. His black beak clasped onto the lichen and tugged it free. Sharp talons of the largest bird grasped a chunk of dry sap bulging from the bark and pulled it loose. The two bodies of feathers spun and dropped their finds on the path. Justine scooped them up and ran her fingertips along the coarse strand and fondled the hardened goop. The flock ascended, peppering the sky with brilliant colors before they disappeared. Beadwork on her leather bag sparkled and long fringes that hung from the bottom danced with the breeze as she unhooked the antler button, tucked the lichen and sap inside and adjusted the braided strap on her neck.

She fixed her sight up the path toward home, turned, and continued toward the scent of a lake. Silence broke. "Rat-tat-tat-rat-tat." Curiosity won out over panic, and she gravitated toward the rapping. Just off the path, a redcrested head of a black woodpecker jerked as he pecked his ivory bill relentlessly into a stump. He swung his head and froze. Beady yellow eyes returned Justine's stare before he spread enormous white-patched wings, lifted into the air, stretched his claws, and slammed them into the stump, sending it rolling toward her. Instinct lifted her foot and halted the stump. A whoosh followed the ascension of the bird. With quivering hands, she scooped up the stump and shoved it into her bag.

Shocked by a loud thrashing noise, she froze, watching a colossal bear charging up the path toward her. Fear rushed through her veins as it stopped in front of her and thrust himself up on hind legs. Extended jaws released a roar past sharp teeth. Her stomach twisted into a knot as his breath warmed her face with a musty scent. His front paws slammed to the ground. In the moments before the dust erupted, creating a wall of swirling dirt between them, their eyes locked. She sank deep into his soft gaze. Calmness engulfed her. When the air cleared, the bear was gone. She pivoted, forcing her sight between the trees.

Without warning, the sun sank. A dull shield washed over the forest and a chill penetrated her bones. She pulled her collar around her neck and zipped her jacket to the top. Shrieks vibrated through the forest followed by a swishing reverberation. Flocks of squawking birds scattered the sky. Whimpering animals scurried. Fear escalated as she spun on the path and scanned the woods. Shadows darted among the trees. Shivers raced up and down her spine. Smells of whisky flashed past while loneliness swirled around her.

The cynical presence, although invisible, was undeniable. With heart thrashing and legs trembling, she ran up the hill toward home.

Justine opened her eyes. Her body shook. She sucked in a deep breath, released it past puffed cheeks, and pushed the afghan aside.

Peeking out at her living room, she crawled from her makeshift cave.

I wish I had someone to talk to about this. Someone who won't have me committed.

With lips puckered, she held her auburn hair back and blew out the candle flame. She gathered up the blankets and flicked on the light switch.

Collapsing onto the couch, she reached for a journal and pencil. Scribbles of the events of her latest journey covered the page. She shook her head, looked up and focused on nothing. Memories of living in fear as a young girl pushed their way into her mind. Visions of cruel men leapt in her thoughts as shame blanketed her like a new layer of skin. A lump grew in her throat. She concentrated on the bear's soft eyes, and her trembling body calmed.

"Damn! Why did I retreat again?" She slapped the arm of the leather couch. "I want to know where that path leads…" Memories of the forest going black, shadows, and the negative presence along with a rush of horror plagued her thoughts but slipped away before they could solidify there.

"Next time."

She tossed her journal on the end table and sauntered to the bathroom, slipped a headband over her hair, and watched her reflection in the mirror. Cleansing cream lathered as she rubbed it on her near wrinkle-free face and wiped the day's makeup off with a warm washcloth. Foam spilled past the toothbrush as she scrubbed her teeth and spat into the sink. She smeared night cream on her skin, said good-night to the pale face with small eyes, and went to her bedroom.

Exhausted, she crawled between the sheets, her mind focused on sleep. She went there.

BACK TO REALITY

Tires screeched as Justine whipped her gleaming Mercedes into the stall between a black Jaguar and a sparkling 300C. She rushed up the stairs and into her office.

"Good morning, Suzan," she chimed as she whizzed past her secretary.

"Good morning, Dr. Cloak, I'll be right in with your coffee."

Justine stepped inside her office, closed the door, and watched her reflection in the mirror peel off her full-length coat. Sunrays reflected off her shiny hair resting on the shoulder pads of her suit that clung to her sleek figure. The notched collar, long cuffs and a center back slit gave it the added chic look to go with her two-inch heels. Ever since her divorce from Ted one year ago, she'd really spiced up her wardrobe. She slid her eel-skin briefcase alongside an oak filing cabinet.

She gazed around the room as she fondled the leather on the edges of her oak desk. Her stare focused on the certificates hanging on the wall. You've come a long way, baby. Uncongealed memories flashed through her mind of struggling in school and her mother's vacant stare. The bear's soft eyes pushed into her thoughts and calmed her.

She laughed out loud, reading each certificate. "Twelve years of postsecondary education, ten years of practicing psychiatry, and I crawl around my living room floor, making caves and—"

Knock-knock.

"Come in," Justine watched the door. Suzan stepped in, balancing a tray filled with the usual, a cup of coffee and a croissant, and set it on the desk.

"Is Shane in yet?" Justine slid into her chair. "Yes, Dr. Moran has been here since 7 a.m. as usual." Justine nodded and smiled.

"Could you schedule a consultation with him, please?"

"Of course."

Justine leaned over her desk and flipped open a leather itinerary. Manicured fingernail tips slid under the dates and times.

"Sanderson cancelled his 10 a.m. appointment, and Moore rescheduled next week's meeting to the end of the month. Croons will be here in a half hour." Suzan opened the door and stepped out.

At 3:00 p.m., Justine pulled her feet up and curled them around to her buttocks, sank into the softness of Shane's leather couch, and pulled her skirt over her knees. Shane undid the buttons on his suit jacket, plopped himself down across from her on a matching chair, kicked off his alligator shoes, stretched his feet over the ottoman, and shook his tie loose.

His secretary placed a tray with two cups of coffee on the table that separated them and left the room.

"So tell me, Justine." Shane's full lips parted in a wide grin. "Are you really puzzled over a case or are you just trying to get me alone?"

She smiled and pulled her personal journal from her briefcase. "You wish."

"Oh" yes I do." His flirtatious chuckle swam through the air.

She frowned at him.

"Okay, I'm sorry. You're just so fun to tease." He sat up and placed his hands on his lap.

She puckered her lips and stared at him.

"Okay, okay." He sank deeper into the chair. "Tell me about the case."

"My patient" Justine coughed the dryness out of her throat "has been having these experiences for about a year. She meditates in a makeshift cave and has these incredible visions."

Justine poured out the whole story in detail while Shane sipped his coffee.

"Has she had any stressful situations that could have triggered this?"

Justine's thoughts flew to the day her husband, now ex-husband, told her he was leaving her for that ditzy woman. Her body weakened.

"She has had relationship problems but seems to have a grip on them."

"Any signs of addiction, eating disorders, alcohol or drug abuse?"

"None. Well, except she is drinking more than usual, but I wouldn't say it's a problem."

"Heart disease or diabetes?"

"No. She has a clean bill of health."

"Self-neglect?"

"No, she takes good care of herself."

"Social life?"

"She has no social life since her breakup."

"Educated?"

"Yes, post-secondary."

His forehead wrinkled. "High-stress job?"

"At times. Yes."

"Speech coherent?"

"Yes, she articulates well."

"Any thoughts of suicide?"

"No. Never."

He looked over the rim of his glasses and tapped his pen on the comments he had scribbled in his notebook.

"Delusional, hallucinations, disturbances in thinking, withdrawal from social activity—come on, Justine, you know this stuff. We are talking a casebook study here of schizophrenia. I recommend you get her started immediately on Clozapine."

Justine coughed into her curled hand. "Clozapine? But the side effect is agranulocytosis." She leaned forward and placed her cup on the rattling saucer, spilling coffee down the sides. Justine's eyes avoided his stare. "That drug causes severe reduction in white blood cells and results in rigorous infection." She took a napkin from the tray and set it between the cup and saucer.

He jerked his hands apart. "Sure, in about one in a hundred patients, and if—"

"Agranulocytosis can be fatal."

He shrugged. "Yes, if not caught early, so that's why you would measure her white blood cell count with a blood test prior to starting treatment and regularly while she receives it and for four weeks after. The results are amazing."

He held his hand out and flipped its palm up. What is it about this patient that has you so wrapped up in her case?"

Justine drew a deep breath. "Except, her speech is coherent. She expresses herself clearly."

Shane's eyes squinted while sipping his coffee.

Justine looked at her notes. "And the so-called hallucinations are in a trance-like state while on an inner journey."

"So-called hallucinations?" Shane's hard stare penetrated Justine.

"She is not confusing these journeys with reality." Her voice weakened.

"Yet, in her reality, she is making a cave in her living room?" He set his cup on the table without breaking eye contact.

"She articulates clearly." He held two curled fingers in the air and tweaked them. "With wildlife while in a makeshift cave." His wrinkled forehead pulled bushy black eyebrows together like a caterpillar over bright green eyes.

Justine's shoulders slumped.

"Why do you think she has a need to be inside a cave?"

"I guess, maybe she feels secure—safer?" "Hmmm, like a child in the womb?" Justine's eyes shot up and met his. "Sounds like she is very insecure."

"I don't think so. Like I said, other than partaking in strange journeys, she appears to be normal."

"Normal according to whom?"

"Touché!"

"I could sit in on one of your sessions with her if you like, assess her in person."

Justine gathered up her journal and tucked it into her briefcase, slid her feet into her shoes and stood.

"Thank you, Shane. I will consider your advice carefully."

"Anytime."

He reached out and touched her on the shoulder. "How are you doing, Justine?"

"I'm doing very well, thank you."

"You look great!"

She smiled. "Thank you."

"I have to say, Justine, you sure handled the whole situation with your ex admirably."

"I've had my moments, but the worst is over."

"Good for you, Justine, you deserve so much better than Ted."

She sighed. "I have to agree."

"Are you seeing anyone?"

"No, but, you know, I think I'm ready to start dating again."

"Maybe we can double date; Kathryn and I, you and your new man."

"Sounds good." Not a chance I'm spending an entire evening watching Kathryn hang all over you, claiming her territory. She's so nauseating.

Justine smiled, reached out, and wrapped her arms around him. "Thank you, Shane." Woodsy cologne swam through her nostrils. His tailored suit, smooth to the touch as his muscular arms squeezed her back. Warmth rushed her soul, increasing her heartbeat.

THE END OF THE PATH

Smoke swirled in the air with a fresh scent as Justine sprinkled loose sage into a shell, lit it and watched as it burned down to a smolder. She turned on her CD player and crawled under the afghan-draped table. Lucent auras swirled her body as she sank deeper, into a spell.

Forest air filled her senses while strolling on the familiar trail. In a flash, an invisible existence of immorality emerged, swallowing all innocence and looming throughout the woods. Loneliness slammed into her, leaving her body trembling with chills. Memories of roaming around an empty home slapped at her. She rushed down the trail and stood in front of a lake. Heat from the sun softened her as she stood before the clear water rippling in the slight breeze. She tilted her head, relishing in the warmth that settled on her face. *I made it. I finally made it to the end of the path, so now what?* Loud clashing broke the silence behind her. She spun. Muscles bulged under fur of the bear charging down the path. He skidded to a stop and plunked in front of her. Fear pulsated through her veins until she looked into his eyes. Peace washed over her. Confusion lingered. A lump rose in her throat. Weakness dragged her to her knees, and she wrapped her arms around his neck. "Thank you for coming back." Her own words and tears puzzled her. The bear nuzzled his head against her, making purring noises, filling her with courage. She stood tall, placed her hand on his shoulder and gazed across the body of water at an island.

The bear nudged her with his forehead.

"Go in the water?" She stared at him.

Prodding her with his nose, he pushed her toward the lake.

She sloshed through until the tepid waters rose to her chest, then thrust herself in and swam toward the island with the bear next to her.

Long tangles of tree roots dangled from eroding soil at the edge of the land. Slippery ropes slithered between her palms as she clutched them and heaved her body up. Sounds of croaking swung her attention back to the water. A frog leapt from a reed, disappearing into the depths with a splash. She reached over, grabbed the reed, shook the excess moisture off, and tucked it into her bag. Water slid from her and pooled on the powdery soil. She squinted and stretched her neck toward the dark forest. Shadows lurched and retreated. Familiar scents of putrid sweat and whiskey breath flashed past her in the breeze. Humiliation boiled inside and restricted her breathing.

Rustles of dry grass took Justine's attention to the bear waiting for her. She glanced at the forest and then scrambled to catch up. The bear stopped in front of a mound, then pushed shrubs out of the way with his nose.

She peered in at the darkness.

The bear lumbered just inside the cave then sat and looked at her.

"You want me to go in there?" His shining eyes from the darkness calmed her. She crouched and entered the cave, and the bear stepped out.

Muted drumming and chanting resonated from further inside. Using her hands to guide her against the cool walls, she followed the narrow maze toward the sound until she came to a wide area with a waterfall tumbling into a rugged hole. She squinted at a figure in front of her, drawing it into focus. Long black braids twisted to the waist of the male native who sat cross-legged on a woven mat. His fingertips slapped and palms thumped on the skin of a drum. Sheathed in a long suede smock and matching pants, he chanted in time to the beat. He pounded harder and faster; his vigorous chanting matching the intensity of the beating of the drum. Swarms of bats flapped past her toward the entrance. She cowered against the wall and covered her head with her hands. Disturbed dust invaded her nostrils. She sneezed. The beating stopped.

Dark brown eyes smiling with pleasure penetrated hers. A deep voice echoed against the jagged walls. "You finally made it."

He reached over and picked up a rock etched with deep erosion, dipped it into a pool of water behind him, and handed it to her.

"Excuse—" She swallowed and coughed past the dryness in her throat. "Excuse me? Finally made it?" He jerked his head toward the cup.

She hesitated, took the rock mug, lifted it to her lips, and soothed her throat.

"Thank you."

He nodded. "I've been waiting for you." Confusion swarmed her.

He stretched his arm palm up toward the mat across from him.

She squatted and sat without taking her eyes off of him.

He held his hand flat, palm facing her. "My name…is Kitchamia"

She paused before her hand mirrored his.

"My name is Doctor—Justine."

Shivers sent goose bumps over her skin. She wrapped her arms around her damp shirt.

He tweaked his head toward her bag. She looked down at the sack, lifted the strap over her head, and handed it to him. He shook his head. She rifled through it and pulled out the strand of lichen and held it up.

He nodded and took it from her, laid it on the ground and twirled a piece of wood between his palms next to it. Sparks jumped to the lichen and smouldered. With puckered lips, he blew until it burst into a flame. He placed it in a circle of rocks and piled small, then larger branches and wood on it.

Flames licked at her hands stretched over the blaze that lifted the darkness in the cavern. Warmth penetrated her and the heat flushed her face.

He broke the silence. "I am pleased you rekindled with Karmas."

"Karmas?"

"Your power animal."

"My what? The bear?"

He nodded. "Karmas has waited a long time for your return; we all have."

"My return? Where was I?" Her world tilted.

"You tell me."

She stared. *I don't even know where I am now, never mind where I've been.*

He reached into the fire with a flat stick, pulled out a hot coal, and set it on a smooth rock. Deep brown eyes looked at her and nodded toward the sack. She reached in and pulled out the hunk of sap, paused and tossed it to him. Leather-like fingers clasped the dry goop in midair. Strong hands ripped it in two and dropped half of it on a hot coal, the remainder inside a natural depression of a rock next to the fire. Smoke swirled into the air followed by a powerful scent of fresh pine. He closed his eyes and breathed deep, pulling the smoke toward him with cupped hands.

Profound eyes looked at her then at the sack. She reached in, retrieved the stump, and rolled it toward him. He scooped it up, filled the hollow with burning coals, and focused on her. Her hands searched the bag until her fingertips found the hollow reed at the bottom.

She walked around the flames, passed him the tube, and squatted next to him. She watched as he placed it between his lips and blew into the smouldering log, provoking an inferno. Flames swelled, danced, and parted inside the stump. He's controlling the burn, but why? She studied his technique.

He flipped the log and dumped out the coals. Flurries of sparks and burning embers scattered across the rock floor. Muscular arms flexed as he scraped the inside with a sharp rock, popped out the bottom, tapped the burnt shavings onto the ground, set the rim on a large rough rock, ground it smooth, turned it over and repeated the process on the other rim. Sap dripped from a leaf he used as a glove to scoop the softened sap from next to the fire. Inside the stump, he smeared it over all cracks. She scrutinized his every move. He pulled a piece of rawhide from the water, took a knife from a sheath and sliced two pieces a bit bigger than the stump.

Her eyes flicked from his face to his hands. He placed the leather back-to-back and punched holes through both with his knife all the way around. Steady hands centered the bottom end of the hollow stump over the rawhide and placed the other one on the top rim. With the holes of both membranes aligned, he threaded rope through all of the punctures, pulled the cord tight and tied it together.

Twirling the creation in his hands, he grinned and tossed it to her. She caught it between her palms, tucked it between her knees and proceeded to pound out a rhythm with her fingertips against the pelt.

He grabbed his drum and pounded in harmony. She followed his lead and imitated his deep raspy voice.

They slapped their drums harder with each passing second and chanted with the same intensity. Peace forced its way inside her. Tears pooled in her eyes and slid down her hot cheeks. Kitchamia lifted his hands in the air, swaying in time to the music while she preformed a solo. The tingling in her hands swept through her body. Droplets of sweat slid over her eyebrows. Thick fluttering eyelashes pulled the moisture in with her tears. Her breathing quickened, breasts heaved, muscles tightened and expanded.

Dizziness swam in her head. An enigmatic sensual tone escaped her lips. She tilted her head back, swaying her body and thrusting her shoulders with each slap of the drum. Her body pulsated down to a quiver as she tempered to a slight slapping on the skin. A soft hum lingered her throat.

Cool, pine-flavored air filled her lungs, soothing her pounding heart. Sweat smeared under her trembling hand as she rubbed her heated face. She stared into his satisfied eyes. Her lips parted but only a squeak came out.

"Take your time." He smiled.

She pulled in and released an agitated breath. Her quivering body calmed, panting subdued and vertigo lifted.

Wow!

"It's time to go," Kitchamia stood.

"But I have so many questions."

"Only you can answer the questions."

"What do you mean?"

"It's time to go now."

"The silhouettes that I see glimpses of in the forest, at least tell me what that is."

"Thy Shadow Self."

Fear gathered and dropped to the pit of her stomach. "What does that mean, Shadow Self?"

"When you're ready to know, you'll not need to ask."

"But I want to know now."

"All in good time."

She fidgeted, stood and draped her bag strap over her head. "All right. Thank you."

Warmth from his strong hand penetrated her back as he walked her to the entrance of the cave where Karmas stood waiting. Perched on a nearby stump sat a large eagle. The sun glistened off of his white capped head and highlighted his singed feathers. His beady eyes held Justine's gaze before he lifted and took flight. Dark outside edges enhanced a large white feather that fluttered to the ground. Justine shaded her eyes with a quivering palm and watched the eagle soar and disappear. She bent, picked up the feather, and slid it into her pouch and walked with Karmas back to the lake.

They jumped into the warm water and swam to shore. The wide span of the eagle's wings blocked the sun as it glided above them. Beady eyes of a black squirrel locked into hers as she pulled herself to land. The squirrel rushed to a nearby bush with silvery leaves.

He pushed the leaves up with his head, plucked the plump silver beads with his tiny claws, and stuffed them into his mouth until his cheeks bulged, spat them on the ground, and scurried away. Justine stared down at the shimmering seeds, gathered them, and dropped them into her bag.

Along the path, she gathered lichen and dried sap.

Sickness washed over her as her peripheral vision caught a glimpse of the now familiar black spirit staggering amongst the trees. Shivers and shame layered her body. The shadow vanished then appeared on the other side of the path, disappeared, appeared in front of her and vanished. She spun, her wide eyes searching, heart pounding in her dizzy head. Nothing. Whiskey and vomit scents filled the air and rushed her nostrils. Her hand flew to her face to sooth away the memories of rawness left by abrasive whiskers. Humiliation consumed her body and coated her soul as she scrambled with restricted breathing up the path.

Justine lay entranced on her living room floor. She pushed the afghan aside and crawled out.

"Oh my god!" Both hands covered her face. She flopped into her chair, snapped out the reclining footstool and reached for her journal and pencil. Her hands shook as scribbles of her events covered the page. Her breathing slowed and body stilled. She flipped the book closed and staggered to bed.

THE NIGHTMARE

J
ustine bolted up, shivering from the cold sweat that soaked her sheets. Her heart thrashed. She looked at the clock: 3:00 a.m. "It was so real!" She relived the nightmare:

Fresh scent of cedar had breezed through the air when she flipped open the lid of a wooden chest and placed the folded afghan inside. Shaman books, candles, smudges and resins dropped on top of the blanket. She smacked the lid closed. A strange sensation solidified inside her.

She flopped onto her chair and kicked out the footrest, breathed deep, exhaled and closed her eyes. Before she could contemplate anything, white lights swirled around her. The room spun. She fought the gravitational pull into the trance, trying in vain to pull herself from the spell. Her physical arms and legs flailed in retaliation until she stood once again in the woods. She ran up the path but slammed into an invisible wall after a few steps, turned and ran down the path with her body stinging.

"Welcome home," grunted Karmas as he pulled his huge head from the bush of berries.

"This is not my home!" she cried, running past him.

"Now it is." He buried his head in the bush.

"Welcome home!" repeated throughout the dismal forest from all the natural inhabitants. She ran faster.

She plunged into the lake, scrambled onto the island, rushed toward the cave and fumbled through the dark maze.

"Kitchamia! Kitchamia!"

"Ahh you made it at last. I've been waiting for you." Kitchamia did not look up.

"What's going on? How do I stop this?"

"When you are ready to know, you will not need to ask." His chanting echoed in time with the beat as he pounded harder and faster on his drum.

She sank to the floor, coiled and shook with sobs. "I'm not staying…I'm not!"

The dream switched to a door slamming followed by the loud click of the lock. It still echoed in her eardrums. Long sleeves of a white jacket wrapped her arms snug around herself. She struggled until exhaustion prevailed.

Justine threw the covers off her and thrust her feet onto the cold floor, shuffled to the kitchen and plugged in the teakettle.

"I need a sabbatical." She dropped a teabag in a mug. "I can't keep doing this."

HOLDING IT TOGETHER

Justine's vision blurred. Her darting screensaver broke her stare: 5:25 p.m.

Thank god I have Suzan to type and file these. She stacked her day's reports in a neat pile and covered them with her favorite paperweight. Her fingertips fondled the huge chunk of shellacked coal and the engraving on the limber pine base. Crowsnest Pass. Memories surfaced of the patient who had given it to her. He brought it back from some little town, an old coal mining community in the mountains. She smiled, recalling his excitement and sense of peace each time he returned from there. He was the one who gave me my first book on meditating. It was supposed to give me a better understanding of what he was about. "I wonder what happened to him?" She laughed out loud. He would probably think I'm crazy now if he knew how far I had taken meditation or how far mediation has taken me. Her body sizzled with apprehension as she drew comparisons between his hallucinations and her experiences under her coffee table. I gave him medication. Her mind raced through all of the prescriptions she had written over the years.

Behind the closed door, she drew a deep breath, pulled her shoulders back, lifted her head, flung the door open and hurried out into the hallway past Shane. He grabbed her by the arm and swung her around to face him. "Whoa, Justine, slow down."

"Hi, Shane, sorry, I just—"

"It's okay, how are you?" His eyes glowed with concern.

"I'm very well, thank you. How are you?"

"Great, just great, I suppose you heard the office gossip?"

"Gossip? What are they saying about me now?" I thought Ted's affair was old news already.

"Well, it's about me, and it's actually true this time. Kathryn left me."

Justine reached out and touched his arm. "Shane, I'm so sorry."

He lifted both shoulders. "I guess it's true what they say about workaholics. In the end, we curl up with our work."

Justine wrapped her arms around him and gave a quick squeeze.

Snickers and whispers followed their secretaries scurrying past them.

Justine pulled away. "I think we just started another rumour."

Shane forced a laugh.

She patted his shoulder and walked away. His scent lingering in her soul.

"Justine."

She stopped and turned. "Yes?"

"Would you like to join me for dinner tonight? A business dinner. We could discuss your patient who crawls around on her living room floor."

"Shane, I'm sorry. I have plans." To crawl around on my living room floor. "I—"

"No problem, maybe another time. Good night, Justine."

The numbers in her dashboard flipped to 9:45 a.m. Justine steered the car into her parking space and rushed into the building.

"Good morning, Suzan."

"Good morning, Dr. Cloak. Coffee is just about ready."

Justine sat in her chair, rolled it to her desk, turned on her computer, and peered at her day's agenda. Suzan is so efficient.

10:00 a.m.—bipolar, 11:30 a.m.—schizophrenia disorder, 2:30 p.m.—posttraumatic stress disorder, 4:30 p.m.— anxiety and depression.

She pulled in a deep breath of air and released it past puffed cheeks. Another day.

Suzan tapped on the door and opened it. "Your four-thirty is here."

Mrs. Swanson's fat feet oozing between the straps of her high-heel shoes stepped into the room. She flipped off a mink shawl. Her short pudgy legs hurried to the couch. Justine glanced at her patient's swollen eyes and blotchy face.

"Mrs. Swanson, it's good to see you, please have a seat." Justine held her hand out toward the couch across from her. Mrs. Swanson's oversized rump plopped into the sofa. She pressed her tight suit jacket with an open hand and twisted large diamonds around her bloated fingers.

"How are you, dear?" Mrs Swanson batted her lashes. "I am very well, Mrs. Swanson, how have you been?" Mrs. Swanson's chubby face lifted with her smile. Her teary eyes searched Justine's. "Please, dear, call me Cassandra."

Justine shifted her weight in her chair.

"We have spent so much time together. I feel like we are friends."

"I'm eager to hear about your week, Mrs. Swanson." Justine leaned over her notebook with pen in hand. "But first, tell me, how the medication is working for you?"

"I'm not so sure this is the drug for me." She pulled off her thick-framed glasses and squeezed the lenses between her hankie and rubbed. "It definitely takes the edge off. The pain is bearable, and my emotions aren't erupting as often…" Her gold bracelets clanged as she adjusted them. "But nor is my sexual drive, and I'm usually quite…dynamic in the bedroom."

Justine forced herself to keep eye contact. Don't laugh, don't you dare laugh. "Yes, that can be a side effect of Paxil."

"I seem to have no passion for anything."

"Don't get discouraged. Remember we talked about this? Antidepressants take time to take effect. Sometimes two to four weeks after treatment is started." Justine scribbled in her notebook. "Once the medication is working to full capacity, you should find yourself able to enjoy life." She leaned forward. "It's important that you continue for at least another two weeks." She tapped her pen on her notes.

"If you do not respond accordingly, we will adjust the dosage. Treatment of depression is an ongoing process."

Mrs. Swanson drew in an agitated breath and nodded.

A series of flashes zipped across the computer screen—an incoming e-mail from Suzan. Her hourly reminder broke Justine's dazed state. She glanced up. The hands on the wall clock pointed to 5:15. She hadn't heard much for the last half hour.

Mrs. Swanson dabbed her soggy tissue under her swollen eyes. "Thank you, Dr. Cloak." She pulled a dry tissue from the box on the table and blew her sniffles into it. "I swear you are the only thing keeping me sane."

"You are who is keeping you sane."

Cassandra ripped out another tissue and twisted it between her fingers.

"Well, Mrs. Swanson, time is just about up. Justine hesitated for just a second then scribbled across a paper, ripped it from the pad, and handed it to her. "Here is a refill for Paxil. I am very pleased with your progress." Justine stood. "I know it's a slow process, but I see definite improvements." She walked to the door, opened it and stepped back, evading the hug she knew Mrs. Swanson craved. The same way she avoided the embrace all her patients yearned for. "Good night, Mrs. Swanson, I'll see you next week."

"Yes, next week. I have so much more to tell you." Mrs. Swanson stepped into the hallway. "Good night, Dr. Cloak, and thank you again."

Justine followed the closing door and leaned into it. She released a long sigh. How did I get here? Forty-five, single, spending my days surrounded by negative energy and listening to people's problems. There has to be more to life. She shuffled to her desk. Oh God, Buddah, or whoever, if there is any hope for me, just give me a sign. Her day's notes compressed under the coal paperweight she plunked on them. Tomorrow's itinerary stared back at her. Prickles formed in her throat. I don't know how much longer I'm going to be able to do this. She flicked off her computer, grabbed her coat, pushed her arms into the satin-lined sleeves, hurried out the door and slammed into Shane's solid chest. The woodsy scent of his cologne filled her senses and worked her body like an aphrodisiac. His strong hands gripped her arms.

"Whoa, Justine, what's the hurry?" He pulled her close. "If you want me that bad, like right here, right now, then okay. But I have to warn you, people will talk."

She pulled away and slapped his smooth shirt. "In your dreams!"

"Every night." His eyes sparkled, bushy eyebrows lifted up and down.

She laughed out loud. "Shane, I'm sorry, I've just had a long day."

"Me too, what do you say we get some dinner?"

"Shane, I—"

"I won't take no for an answer." He placed his arm around her shoulder and steered her towards the door.

She smiled. "Well, I guess we do have to eat." Warmth from his hand penetrated her shoulder.

Zesty spices filled the air. Waiters balancing trays of drinks and food rushed past laughing and chatting patrons. Shane rested his hand on Justine's back and followed the hostess through the dimly lit restaurant. Justine slid into the booth across from Shane.

"May I have your waiter bring you something from the bar?" The hostess slid two menus on the table.

"I'll have a Chivas neat, and I believe the lady will have hers on rocks pressed with a twist." Shane lifted his eyebrows at Justine.

Justine smiled and nodded. "Make mine a double."

"Make them both a double."

Justine squinted at the fine print on the menu, frowned and looked up at the lack of lighting. "I'll have the special." *Whatever that is.*

The waiter set the scotch on the table.

Shane handed him the menus. "Two specials please."

The waiter nodded and left. Justine and Shane clinked their raised goblets. Her neck muscles relaxed, and she melted into her seat, finishing the last of her drink.

"Thanks, Shane, for insisting I come out. I needed this."

"I thought so. You seem really preoccupied and rushed lately."

She sat back. The waiter placed another drink in front of them.

"Shane, do you ever not hear your patients?"

"Not hear them?" His eyebrows pulled together.vw

"Today—actually, for the last month, I find I daydream through most of my sessions." Warmth flushed her cheeks. "I can't believe I just admitted that." She covered her face with her palms.

Shane snickered. "It can get pretty monotonous at times."

"I think I need a sabbatical."

"Maybe I can help you with your workload. God knows I have some spare time on my hands now that—"

"Shane—"

"Now that Kathryn left me." Shane swigged the last of his drink. "Actually, I'm fine. I really am. We had become nothing more than a habit for each other anyway."

She cleared her throat. "I would really appreciate if you could take some of my patients."

He sat back in his chair and nodded. "Back to business, as usual."

She looked down and rotated the glass between her fingers.

He reached out and touched her hand. Heat surged up her arm and around her shoulders.

"Relax, Justine, I know you don't date colleagues." He shrugged. "My loss."

She looked into his emerald eyes.

"I would love to take over the schizoaffective disorder that makes caves in her living room."

She pulled her shoulders back. "I have yet to make that diagnosis of her."

"Come on, Justine, what kind of a nut crawls around on her living room floor and makes a cave under her coffee table?"

She concentrated on mixing her ice cubes with the swivel stick.

"What does she do for a living?"

Justine looked to the left. "She's a medical doctor."

"Whoa, ho." Shane threw his head back and chuckled. "This just keeps getting better."

"My verdict is still out." Her lips stretched tight. "There is something different about her."

"And what advice do you think she would have for a patient of hers that was behaving the way she is?"

Justine shrugged. "I'm not sure she is even going to pursue treatment."

"My god, I hope she does. She needs some serious help."

"I'm not so sure."

"Trances, collaborating with wild animals. Justine?"

He dabbed the corners of his mouth and tossed his napkin onto his empty plate, tipped the last of his drink between his lips and stared at her. "But hey, what do I know? I'm just a janitor."

Justine grinned back at him.

"I suppose you're right. Thank you, Shane." She dropped her napkin onto her half-full plate. The waiter reached over and pulled the dishes from the table.

Her mind raced. Do I need serious help? Maybe if I just lessen my load. "If you can take my bipolar and anxiety slash depression" She stared into space. "I could cut my days in half, maybe even finish compiling my research on antidepressant drugs and put out a report."

He lifted his shoulders and let them fall. "Sure, I can do that. I'd rather have the interesting one but I suppose you would too." He grinned. "Will you at least keep me informed on the Cave Doctor?"

"Sure."

Justine reached for the bill as did Shane. His hand brushed against hers, sending hot shivers through her body. "My treat, you can buy next time." Next time?

KITCHAMIA

Justine lay under her coffee table and breathed in the light, raced down the path and sloshed into the lake until it swirled around her waist. She dove under and opened her eyes wide, pleased to see Karmas swimming next to her. She clambered onto dry land, rushed toward the cave, scrambled inside and stood in front of Kitchamia.

He looked up, his dazzling eyes focused on her, yet he continued to pound his drum.

She scooped up her drum, squatted and tucked it between her thighs. Her hands pulsated, matching his escalating speed slap for slap. The sound amplified and filled the cave. All thoughts vanished. Her head dizzied, heart thrashed, and breathing quickened. A warm purple glow filled her senses; her body grew stronger on the outside yet quivered on the inside. Hands walloped and whacked the hides in synchrony with her vibrating heart. Sweat rolled down her forehead. They stopped. A hush swathed the grotto. Her hands and arms tingled.

Calmness reigned. His stare shifted to her sack. She lifted the strap over her head and rummaged through the bag. Pulling out a handful of seeds, she placed them in his cupped palms. Holding his hands close to the ground, he funnelled the pile in front of him, stood, walked over to the pool jumped in and disappeared.

Flushed with bewilderment, she walked toward the pool. She stood gawking for a few seconds, watching him sink, then jumped in and plummeted. He waited for her with puffed cheeks and fanning hands and feet before swimming away. Pushing the gravity of the water away with her hands, she propelled herself by kicking her feet and followed him in the clear water through a long narrow tunnel of glimmering crystals. A school of bright-colored fish; striped, spotted, and speckled with rainbow shades parted as they swam through. Curly, spiked coral, alive with fiery colors, lined the sandy bottom.

They pushed to an opening and popped their heads into the warm atmosphere. Fresh oxygen relieved her lungs. She pivoted while treading water, taking in the lush jungle that surrounded them. Vibrant shades of greens sprouted from every inch of the soil. The air resonated with the chirping of birds and squealing of animals.

She breathed in the fresh aroma, swam to the edge and rushed to catch up with Kitchamia, who had already started his trek up a steep hill bursting with an array of vibrant flowers and plants. He bent and picked up a bone the size of his index finger, held it close to his squinting eyes and handed it to her. She tucked it into her bag and scurried to keep up. Brilliant yellow flowers burst from a huge plant buzzing with hummingbirds and insects. He stopped and examined the plant then pulled, slow and steady, the sharp spine from the end of the leaf. Strong thin fibres dangled from his fingertips before he passed them to her.

She twirled them into a ball around her finger and stuffed them into her pack. Without warning, coolness washed over the humid forest. The bright sky shifted to a pale gray. Goose bumps crusted her skin. Glimpses of a shadow darting among the undergrowth captured her attention. Vomit rose in her throat. Scents of stale whiskey and sweat filled her nostrils. Her head spun toward Kitchamia.

He returned her stare. "Thy Shadow Self."

Panic chased Justine to the water; she jumped in and swam hard to the cave opening. She scrambled out of the pool and rushed to the fire. Heat from the flames calmed her quivering. Kitchamia's head bobbed out of the pool. He dragged himself out and stood with water slithering off him to the cave floor.

He extended his hand toward the mat. She sat. He nodded and held out his hand.

Rummaging through the sack, her trembling fingers found the small bone and placed it in his palm. "Aren't you going to say anything about what just happened?"

"There's nothing to say. What happened, happened." He rolled and rubbed the bone against a chunk of sandstone.

Confusion filled her mind. "What did happen? Why was I so afraid all of a sudden?"

He stuck a sharp end of flint into the top of the smooth thin bone, pressed, and twisted until a piece of the rock popped out the other side. "When you're ready to know, you'll not need to ask."

With his knife, he whittled the opposite end of the bone into a razor-sharp point. She pulled the ball of string from her pack and passed it to him. Smiling, he threaded the new needle and set it beside him. He picked up a silver seed from the pile and pinched it between his fingers. The powdery shell slipped off, exposing a pale stone. Together, they removed the outer casing from all of the pits. He pushed his needle into each kernel and slid it down the thread before adding another. He dangled the string of oval beads, flipped the ends together, coupled them, then placed the circle of beads over her head and around her neck.

"Thank you."

"It's time to go." Sturdy hands pulled her up. They walked to the entrance, where Karmas waited and walked with her across the island. Shadows of the eagle soaring overhead cast a darkness on them as they swam to shore.

Justine opened her eyes and lay still for a long time, reliving in her mind what had taken place. She reached for the necklace, surprised for a moment that it was not there. *Am I going crazy?* She released a deep sigh and crawled out from under her coffee table.

THE BREAKING POINT

Justine pulled her car into her parking space just as the numbers on the clock flipped to 9:59. She shambled out of the car into the building and up the stairs.

"Good morning, Dr. Cloak, I'll be right in with your coffee."

Justine stopped and turned. "Oh, I'm sorry. Good morning, Suzan."

"Your posttraumatic will be here anytime."

Mr. Rustler twisted his wedding ring around his finger and held his quivering lip with his top teeth.

"Are you sleeping any better at nights?" Justine looked up from her notebook. His eyes drooped. He scraped his jagged fingernails over his scruffy beard and shrugged.

"Maybe in fifteen minute intervals. I see her in every dream, screaming for help." He combed his fingers through his greasy hair.

"Tell me what happens in your dream."

"Nothing!" He stood and paced. "I don't want to talk about my dreams."

"Okay, then we won't." A heavy silence hung between them. "Tell me about your children."

He shook his head. "They invite me over for dinner, but…I don't go." He stared out the window. "We just don't have much in common now that their mother is dead!" He pressed his fist to his mouth. Red rolled up his scrunched face. "How could I have saved myself and not her?" He flopped on the couch and gazed at the floor.

Justine stared at him. I don't know. How could you have?

"Tell me about that day before the fire started."

His clenched hand slammed the arm of the couch; dust particles swirled through the sunbeam that divided the room. "Why am I so damn weak?" The volume of his voice increased. "Why can't I remember getting myself out of the burning house?"

Because you are a hypocrite. You left her sleeping and ran out without even warning her.

He stood and stomped across the room.

"Mr. Rustler." She heard her own soft voice in the room. "Posttraumatic stress is not a sign of weakness." She stared past her patient and recited the words she knew by heart. "These memories are painful, so it's very natural to want to avoid them. But suppressing them is an exhausting fulltime job. You won't be able to avoid them forever. They will emerge under stress or whenever you let down your guard. The sooner we can deal with them, the sooner you will be able to live life to the fullest again."

"This psychobabble isn't helping. I should just put a gun in my mouth and get it over with already."

"Mr. Rustler." She brought the harshness of her voice under control. "Don't be so hard on yourself."

"But you said the drugs would take six to eight weeks to kick in. It's been ten weeks now, and—" He shook his head.

She scanned her notes. Oh my god, it has been ten weeks. I should have adjusted his meds at least two weeks ago. "Not everyone responds to the first type of antidepressant tried." Susan's hourly reminder flashed on the computer screen. Good, time is up. "Let's try you on Prozac. It has proven to be very successful."

"Successful at what?"

In reducing aggression, impulsivity, and suicidal thoughts.

"Successful at increasing the activity of a chemical called serotonin in the brain." Memories of the last time she had prescribed Prozac slammed her thoughts and took them hostage. She recalled Suzan standing in the doorway.

"Dr. Kloak, Mr. Huson's wife called. Her husband shot himself last night. She is coming in for his scheduled appointment on Thursday to talk to you. Your next appointment is…"

On the way home that evening, Justine had swung her car into a bookstore parking lot and rushed inside, looking for anything that would take her mind far away from her job. Maybe a nice juicy romance to get lost in. She found herself flipping through the pages of a book on shamans instead. Customers turned and looked at her when she laughed aloud at the author suggesting modern-day shamans make a cave inside their home under a table instead of risking danger or braving the elements like the ancient shamans did in a real cave.

But despite herself, she set up a cave at home all the while snickering to herself. I'm already meditating. Why not take a little journey? She didn't really believe she would be doing any more than meditating, but the distraction from work was just what she needed. Security blanketed her the moment she crawled into her cave.

It all seems perfectly natural now. What was Mr. Huson's first name? Barry? Barney?

"What makes you think this one will work?" Mr. Rustler demanded.

Justine looked up. Oh my god, did I even finish my sentence? A hard breath escaped her. "Prozac has a reputation for working when other drugs fail."

The memory of Mr. Huson's widow's desperate voice blasted her eardrums as though she were the one sitting across from her.

"You said the Prozac would help him, but he killed himself? How do I explain this to our children?"

Scribbles swirled behind her pen over her prescription pad. "This should ease the pain and eventually help you to feel excited and hopeful again." She ripped the paper from her pad and handed it to Mr. Rustler.

He nodded and reached for it.

They stood at the same time and walked across the room.

She pushed the door open and stepped back.

His desperate eyes held hers. "Thank you, Dr. Cloak. Sometimes I think you are the only one who cares about me. Thank you." He turned and walked away.

Justine closed the door and stared at nothing. A pent up sigh escaped. "Barney. His name was Barney Huson."

Memories filed into her brain like they had a right to be there. She tried to block out the haunting sight of Mr. Huson's pregnant wife sitting across from her. That pale gaunt face with red-rimmed eyes and swollen stomach showed up in Justine's dreams a number of times since then. Justine had controlled the urge to vomit as she listened in detail as Mrs. Huson described, through ghastly sobs, finding her husband dead. The frantic cat clawing at the closed bathroom door and then circling and clawing again. Feral meowing almost louder than the fan on the other side, pushing the bathroom door open with her husband's body wedged against it. Gobs of bloody flesh splattered the mirror walls and ceiling. Just a piece of his beard and chin remained attached to his jaw. Not knowing the screams she heard were her own.

Justine snapped back to the present. "Stop!" She buried her face in her hands. "I did everything I could. Everything I was trained to do."

She stared at the wall covered with certificates. It's not my job to care about these people. Suicides are a reality in my profession. He was only number three or four or— She scanned her memory but could not recall how many of her patients had committed suicide over the years. Not that many.

She grabbed her coat, swung open the door, and rushed past Suzan. "Cancel the rest of my appointments today."

"But Dr. Cloak, you have a full—"

Justine hurried down the stairs and into her car.

Justine crawled into her cave and breathed in the white light. She rushed down the path, Karmas at her side, and past the wildlife. Splashes of warm water hit her face as she sloshed through the lake. Memories of reading that first shaman book swam with her across the lake and once again carried her troubled mind to a more peaceful world. She clambered onto the island, ran through the cave, grabbed her drum and took her ceremonial place across from Kitchamia. Peace filled her; the stress melted away and vanished with the pounding of the drums.

After a long exultant duet, silence reigned.

She pulled the lichen and sap from her bag and laid it on the ground.

He took a sharp rock and excavated dirt, leaving a small hole in the cave floor. He stood, walked over to and jumped into the pool. She drew a deep breath and did the same. She scrambled out of the lake and hurried behind him. He yanked a handful of tall green grass, gathered a bundle of sticks, crammed them into her sack, then dove into the lake. Justine glanced around before jumping in behind him. She pulled herself up into the cave and took her place in front of the crackling fire. *I am where I belong. I'll figure out why I belong here another time.* Her thoughts went back to Kitchamia.

He nodded to her, she pulled the sticks from the sack, created a platform over his trench with them and set fire to it. He placed round smooth rocks over his burning wood.

They watched in silence as the flames hissed and smoked. The sticks gave way and the rocks plummeted into the pit. He reached a flat piece of wood into the pit, pulled out the red sizzling embers and scattered them on the ground.

He looked at her and nodded. She gathered up the lichen and handed it to him. He dipped it into the pool and shook it, sending water droplets in the air. She stood and helped him wash the lichen, tugging out twigs and squeezing it to dampness. He dropped a thick layer of grass over the red-hot rocks. The scent of smouldering grass rose with vapors. He gathered the lichen and packed it in between a bunch of damp grass, lowered it into the pit, and covered it with a substantial layer of greenery. Another grass-scented haze burst into the air. He covered the hole with a flat rock and packed dirt over the top, leaving the surface flush with the ground.

They performed a concert with drumming and chanting. Her mind floated in the tranquility of the cave.

Kitchamia scraped the excess soil from his pit and flipped the flat rock out of the way. He reached in with a stick and pushed the top layer of grass, lifting out a bale and setting it on the floor. He unrolled the grass and removed a solid black loaf, sliced through it with the blade of his knife and handed it to her. She took the slippery sponge and watched him stuff a piece of it in his mouth. She chewed the rubbery, tasteless cuisine and swallowed.

He stood and escorted her to the entrance. Karmas swam with her to shore. The Eagle soared overhead.

Justine opened her eyes and pushed the afghan away. Flipping over onto her hands and knees, she crawled out. She gathered up her ritual aids, flopped onto the couch, and stared at the ceiling. *What does all this mean?* She reached for her journal and pencil and recorded the latest encounter.

THE SABBATICAL

Mrs. swanson stood at the door and blew snot into the white tissue. Her bloodshot eyes gazed like that of a puppy waiting for the approval of its master to jump into his lap. "Thank you so much, dear, thank you." Her hand reached out toward Justine's shoulder.

Justine handed her a dry tissue and stepped back. "I'll see you next week, Mrs. Swanson."

Justine opened her e-mail, created a new message box, addressed it to Shane, marked it confidential, wrote "Transfer files" in the subject line, attached a folder, took a deep breath, let it out and hit Send.

Justine's shoulders relaxed. An incoming e-mail blinked on the screen. She clicked the letter icon and then on Shane's name shining from the inbox. files received prompted on the screen.

Could we discuss them over dinner? ☺

Justine's heart fluttered. She breathed it under control.

Her fingertips flew across the keyboard.

Sorry I have plans.

The curser froze above the Send button. Justine deleted the text and typed in,

Sounds like a plan. 5 p.m. works me. U?

She clicked Send.

Perfect! See you at 5. ☺

Justine shook the ice inside her glass, put it to her lips and swallowed the last of her scotch. She flipped a folder closed and slid it across the table to Shane. "That pretty much covers it. Textbook cases really."

He bent over and slipped the folder inside his briefcase. "Uh-huh, seems pretty uncomplicated. So this leaves you with two patients?"

She separated her clutched hands. "The posttraumatic stress disorder has decided he doesn't need his head shrunk." She tweaked her curled fingers in the air. "So I'm freed right up."

"Except for the Cave Doctor." He grinned.

"Yes, just the Cave Doctor."

"I think this is great, Justine, that you are taking some time for yourself. We should all be so wise."

She gathered her coat and slid out of the booth. "Thanks for your support, Shane."

I hate deceiving him this way, but I need time to explore these visions without anyone's judgment. He'll figure out soon enough that I've taken an indefinite leave of absence.

His warm hand rested on her shoulder as they wove among the waiters and patrons and stepped outside.

She pulled her feet into the car and put the key in the ignition. "Good night, Shane, and thanks again for taking over my patients."

"No problem. See you tomorrow."

She watched him through her rearview mirror, drew a deep breath, and pulled in the memory of his scent.

One psychic experience blurred with the next. Confusion lingered after each journey and taunted her intellect. The constant replay of the journeys in her wakened state distorted her concentration in the physical world. The blankets in her make-do cave became her bed. Nights, days and time now held no significance as she wandered around her home and crawled time after time into her grotto.

Justine hurried toward the ringing phone while tying the belt around her housecoat.

She stood frozen with her heart skipping beats as she glanced down at the call display lighting up Shane's name and number.

"Hello."

"Hi, Justine, it's Shane."

"Oh hi, Shane, how are you?" Her heart beat faster.

"Well, I'm fine. The real question is how are you?"

She shook her head. Focus, Justine. Focus. "I'm wonderful, thank you."

"I spoke with Suzan, and she said you weren't coming back until further notice."

"That's right."

"Justine, are you okay?"

"Shane"—she forced a giggle— "I'm fine. I just needed some me time."

"Okay, how about dinner tonight."

Oh my god, I haven't eaten anything for days. "Sorry, I have plans." To lie under my coffee table.

"Tomorrow night?"

"Shane, I—"

"I'd like to talk to you about the anxiety slash depression you passed over."

The mention of her real life jolted her and chased the daze from her head.

He cleared his throat. "I think she has a serious crush on me."

"Shane, did you lead her on?" Justine laughed hard.

"Ya, she's my kinda woman all right." He laughed. "All five feet and two hundred pounds."

"I'm thinking you're man enough to handle her." Justine pressed her fingers against her stomach and spoke between her laughter. "Don't let it go to your head. I'm sure she had a crush on me too."

The pair shrieked with laughter.

He regained control first. "So, how about dinner tomorrow?"

He's so much fun. What could it hurt? "Sure, dinner sounds great. I'll meet you at the Grinder at seven." "Seven it is. See you then." His voice deepened. Warmth flooded her.

Their glasses of double scotch clinked before their first swallow.

"So the Cave Doctor decided against therapy?"

Justine stared at her menu. "Yes, yes, she did." Justine glanced at Shane.

He smirked. "Too bad. That was going to be interesting."

He handed the waiter the menus. "Two specials?" He raised his eyebrows and looked at her.

She nodded, and the waiter left.

"Did you see any improvement before she packed in the therapy?"

Justine straightened her spine. "Yes, she made it all the way to the end of the path and meets regularly with her power animal, Karmas, and a native guide named Kitchamia, and—"

Shane's forehead wrinkled and eyes gazed into hers. "I meant, did she improve as far as realizing—"

"Oh, no. I guess she didn't." Warmth swept across her cheeks.

He leaned forward on his elbows. "Tell me about Karmas and Kitchamia."

She couldn't believe her ears as she babbled her story out, still hiding that the Cave Doctor is her but shared every detail. The waiter set two fresh drinks in front of them with their meal. She talked nonstop about the journeys as she pushed the food around the plate with her fork.

Shane kept eye contact as he put one forkful of food in his mouth after the other.

The waiter scooped up Shane's empty plate and looked at Justine. She tossed her napkin over her food and nodded. The waiter grabbed the dish and left.

Shane broke his stare and leaned back in his chair. "Wow, and she got all of that while laying in a trance under her coffee table?"

She nibbled on her lip. "Uh-huh."

"I have to admit I'm intrigued."

"Really?"

"Yes, really." He leaned forward, squinted his eyes and pulled his brows together. "Are the things she learned accurate?"

"Like what?"

"Well, like the drum, is that how you make a drum?" She lifted her shoulders. "I don't know."

"Are there silver berries under the leaves of a bush? If so, can we make a necklace out of them?"

We? "Not sure." She stared at him as his voice grew more intense.

"Is that how you make a steam pit?"

She lifted her hand off the table. "I have no idea."

"Can we make that loaf stuff with lichen?"

We?

"It would be easy enough to place sap on coals to see if it smoulders like incense.

Huh?

"I wonder if there's a yellow flowered plant that has a spine on the leaf that can be used as thread?" He tapped his finger pads against his mouth and stared into space. "I can see how it would be possible to make a needle by grinding a bone on sandstone."

"Whoa, whoa, time out." She waved her palms toward him.

He grew quiet. The two burst into laughter.

"Seriously though, Justine, let's try."

"What? How? Where?"

"We'll drive out to the country and go for a walk through the bush and gather all the supplies she got from the animals and birds."

She wanted to laugh but saw the sincerity in his eyes.

"The Cave Doctor received pretty explicit instructions." He shrugged. "We'll just follow them."

Justine tilted her head and lifted her eyebrows. "If it works out, does that mean she's not crazy?"

Shane faked a chuckle. "I have no idea what that would mean."

"Okay, let's do it! How fun would that be?" She slid her arms into her jacket sleeves and pulled her coat over her shoulders. "How about tomorrow?" "Okay, it's a date!" A date?

"Why do I see straight jackets in our future?" He sniggered and slid out of the booth, pulling on his coat.

Her nightmare of being in a straightjacket flashed through her mind and sent chills crawling down her spine.

He draped his arm around her shoulder. They walked out of the restaurant and across the parking lot. He opened her car door, and she scooted in.

"I'll pick you up around 10. We might need my four-by-four."

"You have a four-by-four?"

He grinned like a teenager. "See you at 10."

THE QUEST

Justine collapsed into bed and danced with sleep for the next nine hours.

Her eyes shot open at the ringing of the phone. She glanced over at the alarm clock. 8:00 a.m. She reached for the demanding receiver.

"Hello."

"Justine, I looked up that yellow flower on the Internet." She tried to blink the drowsiness from her head and focus.

"I think I found a match. It's called the century plant. It looks like a giant aloe. It's in the agave family and more related to the cactus than to the aloe though."

"Shane?" Her fuzzy head could barely make out who was talking, never mind what he was talking about.

"Oh, ya, sorry, good morning. Anyway, I'm pretty sure that this is the one Kitchamia pulled the thread from."

She swung her feet out of bed and sat on the edge, rubbing her eyes.

"Until recently, it has seemed to be indestructible. Now they are dying, the scientists can't figure out why. Oh, ya, did I mention they're in the Virgin Islands?"

She stood and reached for her housecoat. "Shane—what are you talking about?"

"The plant that Kitchamia got the thread from. It exists! The natives used it for thread! I was up most of the night researching the things the Cave Doctor learned from Kitchamia."

She balanced the receiver snug between her shoulder and ear, pulled on her housecoat, slid her feet into slippers and ambled toward the kitchen.

"I also found the wolf willow bush. It does have silvery berries under their leaves, just as the cave doctor describes."

The aroma of fresh coffee grounds burst into the air as she lifted the lid off the can and scooped the powder into the basket.

"The natives use it to do exactly what he said, make beads out of them. And the steam pit, that is precisely how you make one, and the drum and the lichen loaf. Justine, do you know what this means?"

She poured water through the top filter of the machine and flicked the brew button.

"That you need medication?" She giggled. "I think a double dose of Clozapine and a straight jacket may be in order."

"Justine."

"Please refer to me as Dr. Cloak." She laughed. "I always keep my patient-doctor relationship professional."

"Justine."

"Okay, I'm sorry, I have to admit this is fascinating!" She pulled the pot out, set her mug under the drip and filled it from the carafe. "I'm just surprised that you've taken such an interest."

Silence. "Me too, actually. Anyway, I can't wait to get going today."

"I'm excited about it too." She blew the steam from her coffee and took a sip.

"Do you want to make me breakfast?"

"No. I still have to shower."

"I meant tomorrow morning." His eager voice morphed deep and husky.

Warmth flooded her and she forced a chuckle. "Oh, trust me, we won't be waking up together tomorrow morning."

He chuckled. "Can't blame a guy for trying. I'll be there by 10."

"See you then. Bye."

She rushed toward the knocking on the door, stopped before reaching for the handle and smoothed her snug cashmere sweater over fitted jeans. She swung the door open and hoped she did not gasp out loud as she stood facing the most gorgeous man she'd ever seen. Shane's silver streaked hair seemed to have lost the battle with the wind. The green wool weaving through his brown alpaca sweater coordinated with his eyes. Snug jeans hugged his hips and his scent floated toward her. She breathed deeply.

"Good morning, Shane." She grabbed her coat, pulled the door shut and walked beside him to his truck.

He pulled the door open. She grabbed the handle, stepped onto the side runner bar and lugged herself into the passenger seat of the new truck. Why do men all buy new sports cars or big, stupid, stomper trucks when they get divorced? The subtle smell of new leather and his cologne swarmed within the confines of the vehicle as he slid into his seat and slammed his door closed. She breathed in the spicy air as the buildings and vehicles whizzed past her window and morphed into trees. He clutched the steering wheel with both hands. "I've been itchin' to get this baby into the bush since I got it last month."

Leaving the smooth pavement, he searched the dash before he reached and pushed the four-wheel drive switch. She frowned and clutched the handle over her door. "Maybe you should slow down."

She bounced on the seat with each rut they grazed. The truck bumped and jarred up the gravel road between the tall spruce trees and pulled into a clearing. When she saw his grinning face, a smile crept across hers.

He looked over. "Ready?"

"I guess." Excitement rushed through her as she climbed out of the truck into the fresh forest air. The sun soothed her back.

He held his hand out toward her. "Let's go see if we can get lost."

She slipped her hands in her pocket. "Have you been here before?"

"Nope, never." He dropped his hand.

"Oh great!"

He threw his head back and laughed. "We'll just stay on this path, so all we have to do is follow it back."

"Sounds simple."

She followed close behind him down a well-beaten animal trail. The woods grew denser. She stopped and pointed at the long hairy lichen hanging from the trees. Her heart quickened. "Shane, it's exactly like what—the Cave Doctor saw."

CAMPING

Shane pulled a plastic bag from his pocket and the two tugged the strands from the branches and stuffed them into the sack. "We can make a steam pit and cook this."

"We'd be here all night."

A sheepish grin played across his face. "I brought a tent and sleeping bags."

She stopped and stared. "Shane, are you serious?"

"I am."

"Did you sleep at all last night?"

He shrugged. "About an hour. How about it? Do you want to camp?"

"Shane, I'm not prepared."

His gaze darted to the ground. "I brought everything we need."

"But I have things to do." Visions of her empty apartment danced in her mind.

"Come on, Justine, it'll be fun. We can set up camp and build a fire and a steam pit." His serious eyes held her stare.

"Okay, this is crazy. But I have to admit, it sounds like fun. Lets do it!"

She watched in awe as he dragged a tent, air mattresses, sleeping bags and lawn chairs from the back of his truck.

He grinned as he shook the tent from its sack and flipped the canvas flat on the ground. They walked around it.

"Something's not right." He raked his fingers through his hair and studied the flat tent.

"I think it's upside down." She giggled.

"Hmmm." They flipped it over. He stood looking at it. "Shane, have you ever set up a tent?" "Never." His wide eyes met hers.

"You never went camping as a child?" She suppressed her laughter.

"No. Always wanted to though."

"Oh god, what have I agreed to?" They bent over laughing.

She regained control first. "Well, I used to camp with my parents, but my father always set the tent up."

"Maybe that's why my wife left me."

"Could very well be."

"You won't leave me will you, Justine?"

His ill attempt at looking hopeless only made her laugh harder." Not'til morning anyway." She gathered up the pegs, placed them into the corner loops. "Here, hammer these in."

"Did you bring a hammer?"

She couldn't stop laughing. "My father always forgot the hammer too and tried blaming my mother for it. Grab a rock and start thumping."

He pounded the pegs, securing the tent to the ground. "Grab the pole and pull it through," She pushed the pole through a cloth tunnel on the top.

He did as told.

"Now bend your end down the same time that I do."

Each bent and pushed their ends into the ground, popping up the abode.

He flipped his palms up and extended them toward the tent. "Voila! Our new home."

She shook her head and chuckled. She'd never seen him so excited and childish. His side of the pole flipped up and the tent collapsed. She laughed.

"You have to secure the pole in the loop then into the ground."

"Gotcha!" He saluted her and took his end. Together they erected the tent.

He grabbed the air mattresses, shoved them into the tent and released the latch activating the self-inflation. She tossed sleeping bags on top of each mattress filling with air.

"When did you get all of this stuff?"

"About three years ago." He lifted both shoulders. "I've never used it though."

He stared off into space. "Okay, let's get a fire going."

She gathered dry twigs and placed them inside a circle of rocks he laid, struck a match and tossed it in. Smoke and flames danced with the slight breeze in the darkening sky. "I'll prepare the steam pit." He pulled a shovel from the back of the truck and dug it into the ground.

"Look what I found." She pulled a piece of sap from a tree.

"Here you go." He slid his shovel into the fire, under a red coal and set it on a rock.

The sap blistered as she placed it on the ember. With cupped hands, they fanned the pine-scented smoke toward themselves and grinned.

Squatting next to a clear stream, they sloshed the lichen through the water and tugged out small twigs. She glanced at him. A feeling of déjà vu threatened her sanity. How can this possibly be so familiar?

Warmth filled her soul. They wrapped the lichen tight in oversized leaves and twisted long strands of grass around it and placed it in the pit. He disappeared behind the truck and returned with a huge picnic basket. She threw her head back and laughed. "I can't wait to see what you have in there."

He unhooked the basket, flipped the lid open, lifted two crystal glasses and a bottle of Chivas.

"You thought of everything." She giggled.

"Yup."

Astonishment swarmed through her as she watched him. He rustled inside the basket and pulled out a thermos filled with ice. He dropped a couple of cubes in the glass, broke the seal on the bottle with a twist, poured scotch over the crackling ice, reached back into the basket, pulled out a bottle of spring water, splashed a bit into the glass, unzipped a baggie, pinched out a stand of lemon rind, dropped it into the drink and handed it to her.

She reached for the glass. "Shane, what would you have done if I wouldn't have agreed to camp?"

"Well, for starters, you would never have known I packed all this stuff." Her smile mirrored his as they clinked their glasses together. She leaned back in her chair. Her neck muscles relaxed as the scotch swam through her veins and fire warmed her body. She inhaled the scent of burning wood and looked over to see him staring at her. His eyes sparkled with a new softness and his face flushed.

"This is wonderful. I needed this. Thanks for joining me." He leaned forward, reaching his palms over the fire.

"Me too. You're welcome and thank you." She stood and stretched her arms over her head and rolled her neck. "I still can't believe you did all of this and in such a short time." He sniggered. "Actually, I can't either. I did get pretty excited."

"Why such an interest in the Cave Doctor?" She stared, waiting for his answer.

He focused on his one hand squeezing the color out of the other.

"My grandmother was—" He coughed into his curled hand. "Said to be a shaman. The town's people, even her family, called her crazy or a witch." He sucked in a breath. "It was my drive to become a psychiatrist to help people like my grandmother." He cleared his horse throat. "I wished so many times that someone would've helped her."

Justine sat and leaned forward in her chair, resting her elbows on her knees and chin in her hands.

"But now I'm not so sure psychiatric help was the answer. Honestly, Justine, I question how much we're helping people with these mind-altering drugs."

She pulled her sweater tight and shimmied her chair closer to the fire.

"My grandma, she knew things that she couldn't have known, a lot like your Cave Doctor. She also spoke of communicating with animals. I was young, so my memory is vague on it all. But I swear she saw through people's souls. Where would she have learned that? There was no Internet back then."

She nodded. "I know."

"Justine, I think we are on to something here."

She stared at Shane and tried to remember what he looked like yesterday. She placed her hand on her stomach as it rumbled. He turned and pulled a bucket of precooked chicken from the picnic basket. He grinned.

She laughed. "I don't suppose you have a lavatory in that basket." She stood. "All that scotch seemed like a good idea a while ago."

He reached over to his supply box, grabbed a roll of toilet paper and tossed it to her. "I think I saw flush toilets just behind that tree."

"Ya, right, flush toilet." She caught the roll between her palms and walked behind the bush.

He set a bottle of waterless soap on the rock when she returned. "I think I saw the men's room over here," he said over his shoulder, disappearing into the darkness. She rubbed the disinfectant into her hands before she reached into the bucket of chicken.

She devoured the greasy batter on the drumstick and pulled tender meat off the bone with her fingers before wolfing it down. A slight breeze pushed the warm night air through her hair. He returned and poured more scotch.

"Tell me more about your grandmother." She sipped her drink.

"She was a beautiful person."

Curiosity in Justine stirred as his unfocused stare deepened.

"She loved me."

"I'm sure she did."

"She collected the oddest things."

"Like what?"

"Rocks, roots, feathers, shells, bones, moss, bird's nests, beehives."

"All natural stuff."

"Uh-huh."

"What did she do with them?"

He shrugged. "She just kept them as ornaments, I think.

She made wands, even made her own drum."

"Was she native?"

"No. But one would have thought so by the life she led."

"She sounds like an interesting woman."

"Yes, I have very fond memories of her."

Shane stood. "What do you say we call it a night? We'll have fresh steamed cuisine for breakfast."

The thought of the steamed lichen created more hunger in her as she tossed her chicken bone into the fire. He unzipped the door and they crawled into the humid tent.

Huge human shadows moved across the canvas as the inside shone with the light of the flashlight.

She glared at him. "Turn around."

He turned while she lay on her bed, wiggling out of her pants. He rifled through a bag and tossed her a plaid shirt over his shoulder.

"You did think of everything." She unsnapped her bra, flung it to the side and pulled the shirt over her bare breasts. She tucked her nose inside and breathed deeply the scent she loved.

"Can I turn around now?"

"Uh-huh."

He sat and pulled his sweater over his head, flopped back and slid out of his jeans while laying on his sleeping bag. "Hey, why do you get to look?" His tone teased.

She broke her stare from his muscular chest glistening with sweat. Her gaze crept down to his boxer shorts before shooting up to meet his grin.

"I'm not just some sex object for you to leer at, unless of course you want me to be."

Her chuckle chimed with his. "Relax, your virtue is safe with me." She threw his sweater at him.

They lay on top of their sleeping bags. The sultry air resonated with the high-pitched song of crickets and the occasional hoot of an owl.

"Good night, Shane." "Goodnight, Justine." *Click.* Blackness snuffed out the light. The hot humid air swam in the tent. Sweat slithered between her heaving breasts, erect nipples. His even breathing grew louder and burst into a snore.

THE OLD WOMEN

Justine drew in the soft white light, climbed onto Karmas' back and clutched his fur as he loped down the path with shadows lurking in the forest. She crawled off, dove in, swam across the lake, clambered onto the Island, scrambled through the cave and sat across from Kitchamia.

Kitchamia stood, walked over and kneeled in front of her. He pressed her palms together between his own. Leaning his forehead against hers, he breathed heavy. Shades of purple swam through her mind as he blew a deep intense breath toward her.

The cave tilted as she opened her eyes. She blinked, pulling Kitchamia's blurry face into focus. He stood, walked across the cave and dove into the pool. She rushed over and dropped in after him. They pushed their way to the surface, gasping for air as she spun, treading water; her eyes absorbed the misty jungle. Bright-colored birds squawked, rodents squealed, and monkeys shrieked, creating a symphony resonating in harmony throughout the atmosphere. They gripped and pulled themselves out of the water with the thick green vines draping over the water's edge.

Kitchamia knelt on the ground above a puddle. She joined him and peered into the small mud hole. He dropped his pointer finger into the center. The darkness rushed to the sides, and the murkiness cleared, leaving a vivid display in the center. An image manifested and revealed a small boy, tousled black hair, brown pants just a bit too short, plaid shirt buttoned wrong, walking through the forest, holding the hand of an older woman. Her suede dress dragged against the dusty ground. A sack identical to the one Justine carried in her journeys draped over the old woman's head and hung next to her side. Long gray hair twisted in a knot at the back of her neck. The boy's eyes sparkled as he gazed up at the elderly lady.

Justine squinted and thrust her face closer as the old woman burst into flames. Black smoke billowed into the air, and the boy dropped to the ground, pressed his nostrils shut with his fingers and curled into a fetal position. A deep haunting moan escaped his quivering lips. Convulsions jerked his trembling body as colorful bits of fatty tissues burst from his chest and scattered into the air.

An iridescent form of the old woman swept down and kissed the forehead of the trembling boy before a gust of wind swept her into the sky and out of sight. Justine looked up to see the scattering fragments from the boy's body settling. One pushed its way into a beehive, another into a hole in a tree, and another fluttered into a bird's nest. An eagle with scorched feathers landed softly on the boy and covered him with his wings. The boy's arms and legs flailed until the eagle lifted and flew to a nearby stump. The boy grabbed a handful of rocks and threw them at the bird. He shouted between sobs, "Get out of here! Go! You are not even real! You are just a dumb bird!" The eagle pulled its wings around itself, shielding its body and face, squawking as the rocks hit him and flew away looking more like a vulture than an eagle with its head hanging low. Justine looked up at Kitchamia, hoping her horror was contained, but knew it seeped from her eyes. Kitchamia stood, ran back to the water, and jumped in.

She followed and clambered out of the pool. Kitchamia walked her to the opening of the cave. Her body quivered, watching the ascending eagle with scorched feathers disappear into the sky. She jumped into the lake and swam next to Karmas back to shore.

She froze when she saw a man standing behind a tree.

Justine opened her eyes and stared at the darkness inside the tent, heart thrashing and body quivering. What was that? Who was that? Why did I retreat? Go back! She closed her eyes, pulled in the light, and ran down the path. The man ran toward her.

Justine's eyes shot open. Her body quivered. Who is that? She closed her eyes and tangoed with sleep.

She woke to birds filling the air with song, a crackling fire and the smell of strong coffee brewing. She crawled out of the tent with her pants in her hand.

"Hey, gorgeous. I thought you were going to sleep the day away."

She stood and stretched then pulled her pants on.

He poured the steaming coffee into a mug and handed it to her.

"Thanks."

"Did you sleep well?" "I did, and you?"

"I had the weirdest dreams. I was standing on a path just like the one your Cave Doctor was on. He laughed. "And there was this eagle with burnt feathers."

She wrapped her hands around the cup and blew the steam before taking a sip.

"You were there too. Only every time I waved to you, you ran the other way."

She looked up and returned his stare. Could it be? "Can you blame me?"

He grinned back at her. "It was so real." His voice full of awe.

She tried to concentrate on what he was saying but confusion tumbled through her brain and blurred her thoughts.

Shane pulled the last of the grass off the steam pit and lifted out the mass wrapped in leaves. He parted the greenery. Justine leaned over his shoulder and the two stared down at the black congealed loaf.

His nose wrinkled. "It does not even resemble what we put into the steam pit."

She gasped, "I know. It's exactly the way the Cave Doctor described."

Shane sliced two pieces off and handed one to her.

She nibbled on the tasteless rubbery matter. "It even tastes the way she described!"

"And she learned how to do this while laying under her coffee table?" He pressed the fibrous substance between his fingers and held it to his nose.

She lifted her shoulders and let them drop.

"Are you sure she didn't look it up on the Internet or in a book?"

"Positive!"

"Positive?" He held her stare with his eyes and pushed the piece into his mouth. Her face warmed. "Well, I guess I can't be positive." But I am.

His eyes widened as he chewed. "I've had this before… at my grandmother's, when I was very young."

"Really? How did she know how to make it?"

He shook his head. "I have no idea, she couldn't" He looked at the ground. "read or write." He glanced up. "Someone must have told her but she didn't have any friends or associate with anyone besides us." His forehead creased. "Someone had to have shown her." He shrugged.

"Obviously she had a life that I don't remember." She stared at him with curiosity swelling inside her.

"After breakfast, let's go look for a wolf willow bush and see about making a necklace," He beamed. "I brought a needle and thread just in case."

He pulled a portable barbeque from the back of his truck and fired it up.

She snickered. "Shane, I can't believe you did all of this?"

He shrugged. His eyes sparkling. "I know you weaken on the spur of the moment, so I had to be prepared."

"And how is it you think you know that about me?"

He grinned and yanked a fry pan from the box and set it over the heat, poured grease into it, cracked four eggs and plopped them inside.

She shoved the last bite of egg and bread into her mouth. "Well, that may not have been as interesting as the steamed lichen." She tossed her paper plate into the fire. "But it tasted a whole lot better. Thanks, Shane."

He rubbed his bread over his plate, soaking up the last of his eggs, shoved it in his mouth, and frisbeed his plate into the flames.

"Ready to go exploring?"

She stood. "Let's go!"

They strolled through the stillness with the sun smouldered down and resting on their shoulders. Soft sounds of a stream trickling over rocks in the distance and the nibbling of bark by small animals of the woods soothed their souls.

For the first time, she did not attempt to control the invisible warmth that radiated from him and wrapped around her. If he were to reach for me now, I'd reach back. She watched in awe as he scanned the forest with the seriousness of a secret agent on a mission. Pleasure saturated her and goose bumps popped across her skin as passion surged from inside. Her body quivered, and she yearned to touch him.

He rushed toward a shimmering bush and lifted leaf after leaf, peering under each one.

Fantasies filled her mind; Shane's strong hands on her shoulders walking her backward toward a huge tree and pressing her against the trunk with his body. Breath warms her ear, his voice pleads, "I need you." Smooth lips crush against hers.

"Justine, look!"

Her breath escaped. She hesitated for just a second before joining him at the bush, her body still trembling. She stared at the silver beads identical to the ones the squirrel had given her. "Oh my god!"

Shane pulled a plastic bag from his jeans pocket. They tugged the treasures from the branches and dropped them into the bag.

"I suppose we should get back and start taking down camp," Justine kicked at a rock.

He turned and faced her. "Why?"

She chuckled. But the thoughts of another night in the tent, him reaching out in the darkness, sent a quiver of desire through her.

"No seriously, why?"

"Well, for starters, you have to work in the morning."

He looked away. "I took a month off."

"What? Are you serious?"

"I am. I followed your lead." His eyes searched hers.

"Let's stay another night."

"What about the patients I passed over?"

He shrugged. "Dr. Carlo's wife is pressuring him for a new boat, so he was happy to take on extra patients. So what ya say?"

"Shane I need to—"

"Need to what?" He smiled. "One more night." She laughed. "Shane, I can't just—"

"Why? What do you have to get back to?"

The thought of an empty home and dwindling career filled her mind. She looked up at his hopeful face and laughed.

"Sure, why not?"

"Okay, let's get back to camp and see if these make beads." He shook the bag.

SHANE'S BREAKDOWN

Shane loaded wood onto the smouldering coals. Justine slid the powdery silver off the seeds and stared at the greenish pit. Her hands shook as she threaded a needle and strung a necklace, just as Kitchamia had done for her.

"Hamburgers okay for dinner?"

"You brought hamburgers?" She glanced up.

His smile spread. "And buns and cheese and ketchup." She grinned. "I should probably be afraid of you." The wood burst into red and yellow flames.

He sat down across from her. "So how's the necklace coming?"

She walked over to him and draped it over his neck.

"Hmm." He lifted it and held it in his fingertips. His eyes glistened. "My grandmother wore a necklace just like this."

He stared at it. "It will turn brown after the seeds harden."

"She knew to use the seeds as beads?"

"She must have." His stare deepened. "She knew so much about nature. She was always gathering herbs and making her own medicine, tinctures, and teas."

"Did you ever try any?"

"I remember one time having excruciating abdominal pains. She covered my stomach with clay." Shane looked at the stars. "The pain subsided almost immediately. My father was furious. Said she was ruining the family's reputation with all her crazy witchcraft."

"Really?"

Shane nodded. "He was so mad, I thought I'd done something wrong."

"You were young."

"He gave her an ultimatum to stop the witchcraft or stay away." Shane stood and poked at the fire with a long stick. "We were all she had." A flurry of sparks scattered into the dark sky.

"Did she stop?"

A sheet of gray washed over his face as it twisted and puckered. A stiffened moan escaped his throat. He folded his arms tight against his stomach and tucked his chin into his chest.

Shock consumed Justine as she watched him wither into the memory. His distorted words, barely audible. "The next day…they…found her…burnt body hanging from a tree in the forest."

"Oh my god, Shane!" Justine reached out and wrapped her arms around him. His quaking body slumped against hers. His teeth chattered in her ears. A raw whimper seeped out. He clung tight and shook with sobs. His spicy scent now mixed with smoke from the fire.

He pulled away. His face streaked with tears. "Justine, I'm sorry…I…"

"Oh, Shane, sorry isn't necessary. That must have been so horrible for you."

He drew in a shaky gulp of air. "Worse"—he let out the trembling breath— "than one can imagine." "Do they know who did it?" He shook his head. "Do you think your father—" "No!" His eyes met hers. "Okay. I just thought…"

"I know, so did my mother. I heard her accuse him." Shane choked on his words. "The thought is unbearable to me." He wiped his palms on his jeans, pulled in a deep breath and forced his breathing to a slow even pace. "So anyhow, there you have it, my childhood in a nutshell."

"Shane, I'm so sorry."

He nodded and sat on his chair. He clenched his top teeth over his quavering lip. His shoulders collapsed. He dropped his forehead to his lap and sobbed. Justine dragged her chair in front of his and sat, rubbing her hand on his back and through his hair while he wept. She laid her cheek on his back, overwhelmed with the need to care for and comfort the little boy who suffered such anguish.

Confusion swam through her as she filled with the strong desire to help carry this burden for him. The night sky filled with twinkles as he released turmoil that had been pent up for forty-eight years. Two hours later, his sobs subsided into the odd sniffle.

He sat up, blew his nose into a napkin, and smeared his shirtsleeve over his eyes. "Justine, I'm so sorry, I had no idea that was…"

"Come on, Shane, don't say sorry. I feel privileged that you felt safe enough to share that with me."

"I had totally forgotten about the lynching and burning."

"We both know how trauma amnesia works. A psychological disturbance like that would rock anyone's world, never mind a little boy's." She reached out and squeezed his cold hand.

He forced a smile and squeezed back.

"Did you ever receive any kind of counseling for this?"

He faked a chuckle. "Obviously not." He stood and walked to the cooler and flipped up the lid. "How'bout them hamburgers? You must be starving." His voice still shaky.

"Sure."

The patties sizzled as his quaking hands smacked them on the grill. Aroma of fresh searing beef wafted through the air.

"I just can't believe that I could have suppressed that all these years."

"The mind does what it has to do to protect us."

"But this is my job. It's what I do."

She clutched his shoulder. "We're human, just like the rest."

"But still…oh my god, that poor woman. She was no more a witch than you are."

Justine swallowed past the lump in her throat and attempted to bring her widened eyes under control. "She just had a huge appreciation for nature."

"Sure, and knew how to utilize it." Smoke rose with the scent of barbequed hamburgers as he flipped them over.

"Just like the Cave Doctor." She held her breath and waited for him to answer.

"Yes, but that still doesn't explain how they knew all the stuff they did."

"Does it matter what we call it?"

"What do you mean?"

She looked away. "Divine intervention, intuition, shaman journey… witchcraft?"

"I guess not, but all those imply—" He looked up at her and smirked.

"I know." She stood, rifled through the boxes and coolers and pulled out paper plates and condiments. She parted the buns and slopped them with ketchup, peeled the plastic from the cheese slices and placed them over the searing burgers. He slid the spatula under the meat as the cheese blistered and plopped them onto the buns.

She devoured hers and dabbed at the ketchup that oozed from the bun onto her chin.

He nibbled the first half and tossed the second half into the fire.

"Scotch?" he stood.

"Sure, thanks."

Silence wrapped around them as they sipped their drinks. The air cooled. They both concentrated on the flames as they burned down to glowing embers. "Ready for bed?" Shane looked up.

"Uh-huh."

Silence followed them inside the tent. She removed her clothes and pulled on her nightshirt, dragged her sleeping bag close to his and pulled him into her arms. His warm tears slid down her neck as he shook, darkness absorbing each of his sobs.

Justine's eyes shot open. Last night's vision—that was Shane and his grandmother! I know where the pieces of his fragmented soul are.

Justine opened her eyes. The smell of campfire and sizzling bacon made way through the canvas and into the tent. She unzipped the door and crawled out into the hot air.

"Good morning, beautiful." Shane fidgeted and concentrated on the splattering grease escaping the fry pan.

"Good morning, Shane, how are you feeling today?"

"Justine, I'm so sorry…"

She walked over, wrapped her arms around him, and squeezed tight.

"Shane, don't apologize. I'm glad I was here for you."

He stared toward the sky. "No one has ever been there for me like that." He looked over. His eyes locked with hers. "Thank you."

She smiled and rubbed his shoulder. A bird sang as they ate breakfast. Its sweet melody soothing her soul.

"I suppose we should take down camp." Shane watched his foot push dirt around. "Let's stay."

He looked up. She stared back.

"Really?"

"Really." She grinned. "Do we have any food left?"

"Hamburger buns."

"I'll go back to town, shower and get some supplies." Justine tossed her paper plate into the fire and stood.

"You mean, like, let you drive my truck?" He smiled. "I'll come with you."

"Suit yourself."

Justine hung onto the handle over her shoulder as they bumped along the trail. Silence replaced the clatter, and the vibration under her butt ceased as Shane geared down and steered the truck onto the smooth highway. Dizziness swam in her head as the noise of cars whizzing past assaulted her ears. Gas fumes filled the air, rushed her nostrils and settled into her stomach. The lights, honking horns and screeching tires all spun in her head.

He pulled up in front of her apartment and pushed the gear into park. "Are you okay?"

"Uh? Oh… yes, why?" She opened the door.

"You're suddenly so pale."

"Nothing a quick shower won't take care of."

"Okay, are you sure you want to go back?"

She smiled. "I'm sure. Actually, I'm really sure."

"Okay. I'll go restock our supplies and return."

"See you in a bit." She stepped to the rail and hopped onto the pavement.

She climbed the stairs, aware for the first time of the scent of paint, rug fibers, glues and disinfectants chasing after her. Inside her apartment, stale sage overpowered the synthetic smells but did not conceal them altogether. She walked to the bathroom and twisted the tub taps. Steam rose as she splattered essential oils into her bath filling with soft bubbles. She peeled off her clothes, dropped them to the floor and lowered her body into the warm water. Resting her head on the bath pillow, she closed her eyes and pulled in the pureness of the ylang ylang aroma. She ran her hands over her breasts and between her legs, thinking of Shane. Just as the bath started to cool, she stood and lathered her hair under the hot shower. Standing in front of the foggy mirror, she twisted her wet hair into a towel on top of her head. Loud knocking broke the silence.

She slid her arms into her housecoat and rushed to answer the door while pulling the belt tight and flipping it into a knot.

The door swung open.

"Hey, beautiful." Shane's shaven face smiled at her.

Awareness of her naked body under her housecoat sent shivers rushing over her skin.

"That was quick." She pulled the towel, freeing long stands of damp hair. "I'll be ready in five." She called over her shoulder as she headed toward the bedroom. "Make yourself at home. I'll get dressed."

"Can I watch?"

The thought warmed her body.

"Shut up." She turned and threw the wet towel at him.

The full-length mirror reflected her curves. She wiggled into a pair of jeans and dropped an oversized T-shirt over her bare breasts. She hauled luggage from the closet, plunked it on the bed, pulled T-shirts and shorts from the hangers and dropped them into a suitcase.

"How long are we staying?" she shouted toward the door.

"As long as we want."

She stared at the closed door and then piled more clothes into her case.

"I'm ready."

She lugged her suitcase down the hall. Shane stood and reached for it.

"Thanks."

"You're welcome." He grinned.

God, he's cute.

"You're beautiful with no makeup."

"Oh, I'm sure." She sneered and swiped her palms over her face. "It does feel good to let my skin breath for a change. She pulled the door closed behind them and slipped the key into the deadbolt.

Justine reached for the handle overhead and hung on tight until they pulled up in front of campsite. "We're home," he beamed.

She breathed deep the fresh air. This feels like home.

He reached for her hand. "Let's go for a walk."

She tucked her hands into her jeans pockets. "Sure."

He pulled a plastic bag from his box of supplies and shoved it into his back pocket. "In case we find something we want to bring back."

They sauntered through the dense trail toward an open field. He grabbed her shoulder and nodded toward a large deer and a tiny speckled one. The mother nibbled on a bush while her fawn pranced and bounced around her. Shane pulled Justine by the hand up to a small mound where they sat and watched in silence. The deer wandered into the bush as the sky darkened, clouds parted, and the moon took its place in center sky.

Justine stood and looked down. "Is that sage?"

He shrugged. "Not sure."

She squeezed and rubbed the leaves between her fingers and brought them to her nose. "It is!"

"What does one do with sage?"

"We could make a smudge." "Smudge?"

"It clears away negative energy."

He pulled the bag from his back pocket and opened it up. She plucked the stems and dropped them in.

Startled by a far-off rumble, they looked up and watched in awe as a thundering noise came from the forest. A huge dark mass burst from the blackened trees. The bear's large rump swayed behind him as he charged across the open field. Snorts and sniffles followed his nose through the air. The mass of fur and claws clomped towards a pile of what appeared to be a carcass and gathered it into his mouth. The moon's sheen intensified his coat blended with shades of black hairs tipped with silver. A huge hump protruded from his wide shoulders.

Fear pulsated through Justine. The slight wind delivered the bear's musty scent to her nostrils.

An eagle swooped, grabbed a piece of meat, and flew low to the ground with the bear snarling and chasing after it.

"Let's get back to camp." Shane tweaked his head backward. Justine grabbed his hand and followed close behind.

Once a safe distance away, she spoke, "That was so cool!"

"It was. It really was."

The Curative

The tidy camp lit up under the glow of the full moon. Shane set fire to the kindling and piled bigger pieces of wood over it until huge flames crackled and leapt from the pit.

A tawny owl's round eyes flickered from its perch high in the tree. He clutched the branch with his sharp talons, bracing against the gusts of wind that messed the round ruffs on his flattened face. He tilted his hooked beak and screeched into the night.

Shane slapped two fresh steaks onto the grill. Justine ripped the lettuce, chopped onions, diced tomatoes and dropped them all into a bowl. She poured oil over, sprinkled the salad with salt and pepper and tossed everything together. After dinner, Shane watched as Justine bundled the soft sage and twisted thread around it, securing it into a wand. He held one to his nose and breathed deep. "My grandmother made these too."

Justine smiled at him. She dipped the smudge into the fire, let it burn for just a bit before she blew out the flame. She walked around Shane, pushing the smoke from the smouldering sage toward him.

"Shane?"

"Ya?'

"Do you trust me?"

"I trust you."

She pulled her chair in front of his, placed her palms on his shoulders, and leaned her forehead against his. She closed her eyes and blew a long steady breath toward him. She sat back and held his pressed hands between hers.

"Relax. Breathe in, breathe out. Hear the breeze. Feel the light of the moon entering through the top of your head. It's sinking down through your shoulders and spreads throughout your arms. Gravity pulls it to your chest, into your stomach, down your legs, and into your toes." His body softened next to hers.

"You're walking through a forest. You're seven years old. You're wearing brown pants and plaid shirt. A refreshing breeze sweeps across your ankles with each step. Your small hand is secured inside your grandmother's soft hand." "No!" Shane stiffened and opened his eyes.

"It's okay, Shane, close your eyes, breath in, breath in the white light."

Shane breathed deep land closed his eyes. Tense muscles softened under Justine's hands.

"Your grandmother has something to show you."

Warmth engulfed Justine and fused her soul to Shane's as they watched the vision unfold in front of them. His grandmother stood before him, smiling with opened arms. She walked toward him. He stepped back, stared for a second, then rushed to her and pulled her to his chest. "Grandmother."

The old woman tugged out of his embrace, and cradled his face in her wrinkled hands. "I knew you'd make it."

"Make it? What does all of this mean?"

She crooked her bony finger and walked away. "Come." They followed behind the woman's long flowing gown and watched as she parted some bushes with her elbow. She nodded toward a bird's nest, nudged the robin sitting in it and pulled out a fatty mass of glowing orange light. Compassionate eyes smiled at Shane as she tucked it into her sack. They scurried after the old woman.

Grandmother nodded toward a beehive and placed her hands on either side of it. An iridescent ginger color radiated from her hands toward the nest. A swarm of bees burst out. Her hand morphed into a long stream of gel and she reached into the hole of the nest, pulling out a shimmering glob of blue light. She smiled at Shane and placed it into her sack.

He shook his head, rushed to catch up with his grandmother and wrapped his hand in hers. Justine followed close behind. They walked down a trail until they came to a huge tree vandalized by a woodpecker. Grandmother reached her hand into the hole, moved furry babies out of the way and pulled out a glowing yellow blob. She held it high in the air, smiled at Shane and tucked it into her bag.

"Grandmother, look!" Shane pointed to an eagle with scorched feathers hovering over them.

His Grandmother smiled. "Krimmley. He is so happy that you're back."

"Back?" Shane looked puzzled.

"Krimmley is your power animal."

Visions of that very eagle following her, sifted through Justine's mind.

"My power animal?" Shane stared at the eagle. "Why is he burned?"

Grandmother stopped and smiled up at Krimmley. "He tried so hard to save me from the flames."

"Grandmother…" Shane's voice cracked.

She put her hand on his shoulder."It's over now and I am fine. We need to focus on why we are here."

"But who…?"

"No."

"I need to know; I will bring them to justice"

She took his hands in hers. "It's over now and we need to stay focused on love or we'll lose this magical moment." Leaves on the trees quivered in harmony with her fading flesh.

"Grandmother, stay!"

"Anger and vengeance will interfere with your destiny. Love is the only thing that can move us forward." She turned and motioned for him to follow.

His tense facial muscles softened. Her body intensified. Shane scurried after his grandmother as he looked back at Krimmley.

They continued down the path until they came to a clearing with a fire roaring inside a contained pit of rocks. Grandmother picked up a bundle of sage, dipped it into the flames and walked in a circle around Justine and Shane, waving the smouldering wand. The smoke and scent of sage gravitated toward them and clung to their bodies.

Her open palm waved toward the ground. Justine and Shane sat.

Grandmother walked to Shane, stood over him, placed her bag on the ground and nodded to Justine. Justine stood and pulled the yellow blob from the sack. Warmth penetrated her hands and surged through her. She passed the shimmering light to the grandmother with the care of a mother holding her newborn. The old woman received it with the same reverence and held each shimmering light on the top of Shane's head until it spiralled and absorbed into his skull. Shane jerked. His shoulders pulled back, as his body turned transparent. The last shimmering orb sank to his chest, adhered to the others and completed his soul much like the final piece of a puzzle.

Grandmother pressed his palms together between hers, leaned her forehead into his, blew, pulled her head back and kissed his cheek. She walked over to Justine, wrapped her arms around her and squeezed tight.

The old woman faded before their eyes as a gust of wind swept her up into the sky.

Justine opened her eyes and stared at Shane sitting, tears seeping through his closed lashes, his hands still pressed between hers.

He opened his eyes and blinked. He pulled back and looked at Justine. "What the hell was that?" his voice squeaked.

Justine shrugged. "What was what?" Could it be?

"Where was I?"

"You tell me."

"You and I were walking through a forest with my grandmother. She—"

"Was gathering your fragmented soul and returning it to you."

Shane pushed himself to his feet. "That's what that was?" He spun. "I've never experienced anything like that." His head swung back toward Justine. "You saw it too, right?"

"I did."

"So what does this mean?"

Justine returned his stare. "I'd like you to meet Kitchamia." Fear and embarrassment pulsated through her veins.

Shane's stare deepened. "You know him?" His hands flew apart. His bottom jaw dropped. "You're the Cave Doctor!"

Justine scrunched her face. "Do you still think I need to be medicated?"

"Well, if you do, then so do I." Shane plopped on a log and dropped his face into his hands. "Wow." He looked up. Shock clung to his face like a plastic wrap. He sighed and rubbed both eyes with his palms "How would I get to Kitchamia?"

"Do you trust me?"

Shane blew out a deep breath. "I trust you."

She pulled up a stump and sat across from him. She placed her hands on his shoulder and pressed her forehead to his. A vibrant purple blasted between their skulls. Warm energy surged and connected the two.

"Follow me."

Justine ran like a horse on the home stretch. Shane chased after her down the path. Shadows jumped in the trees.

"Justine wait!"

"Hurry up!" She sloshed through the water and dove in. "Justine!"

They pulled themselves onto the island at the same time. "You're a fast swimmer." She grinned.

"Slow down. This is all new to me."

"Wait, it gets better." She hollered over her shoulder.

She ran to the cave opening then turned and waited for him. He caught up and stood across from her. He stared as though seeing her for the first time.

She chuckled. "Ready?"

"I guess."

She went in first. He followed close behind.

Kitchamia sat beside a roaring fire in a trance-like state. He opened his eyes and smiled.

Shane squinted and pulled Kitchamia into focus. "Oh my god, you're real?"

Kitchamia tilted his head back and laughed. "I've been waiting for you."

Shane's wide eyes met Justine's.

Kitchamia held his hand out, palm up, toward the ground.

The pair sat.

Kitchamia looked at Shane "Nice necklace."

Shane looked down and fingered the beads and smiled back.

Justine opened her mouth.

"I know." Kitchmia smiled. His stare returned to Shane.

"Your grandmother is a beautiful soul."

"You knew her?"

"Knew her? She is my guide."

Flickering shadows danced behind Kitchamia. They materialized into a shimmering form then an iridescent figure of a lady. Shane watched with wide eyes as his grandmother appeared from the lights and shadows. She placed her hands on Kitchamia's shoulders, leaned over him and blew into the top of his head.

Shane leaned toward Justine. "What's she doing?"

"Not sure."

Kitchamia vanished.

Justine and Shane gasped in unison.

"Come." The old woman crooked her finger and walked away.

Chills swept over them as they hunched and scurried behind her further into the dark cave. Black snuffed out all light and dampness washed over Justine. She stopped.

"I can't see." Justine looked back at the soft glow from where they had entered. I should go back.

"You have to trust." Grandmother's soft voice traveled through the air.

"Shane, where are you?" Justine's voice quivered. Fear circled through her. Smells of sweat and whiskey wafted past her. Flashes of being dragged into a dark alley by a drunken man broke the blackness. She squeezed her eyes then opened them wide, relieved to see nothing.

"I'm here." Shane's voice warm, like his hand that settled on her shoulder.

"Shane, I'm scared. I can't see where I'm stepping." He squeezed both her shoulders.

"I can't either, but I trust her. She wouldn't bring us here if it wasn't safe."

"I trust you, Shane."

One hand clutching Shane's, the other flailing in front of her, she took careful steps on the slippery uneven surface. Have to trust, have to trust.

A sliver of light streaked through the blackness. A few more steps. Up ahead a glow crept through the cave. They rounded a corner. A blast of light shone inside, silhouetting the elderly woman crawling into the daylight. Justine focused on it and slipped out of the small opening into the forest. The sun wrapped around Justine and heated the damp that clung to her.

Grandmother stood at the top of a mountain, Shane at her side, looking down into a forest of spruce and pine. Sinister shadows lurked behind and bolted between trees. An eeriness washed over Justine. They trudged through the thick woods. Shane's excitement glowed from his face. His wide eyes shifting from one side of the forest to the other until the trio came to a small clearing. The old woman sat on a log, stared at them, nodded and smiled. "We need a circle of rocks."

They both scoured the surrounding forest, lugged heavy boulders and placed them strategically in a huge circle. Kitchamia and Krimmley emerged from the forest and sat at the edge of the loop.

"Very good. Now we will open sacred space." Grandmother stood and stepped inside the ring.

Justine looked at Shane. "Sacred space?" Shane shrugged.

His grandmother pulled a sage smudge from her sack, struck a match and held it steady until the bundle burst into flames. She blew it out and walked around the loop, chanting and swaying the smouldering sheaf then placed it in a concaved rock. She faced south and reached her hand high in the air.

"To the winds of the South." She closed her eyes and pulled in a deep slow breath through her nostrils and released it through puckered lips.

The old woman stood tall as she turned and acknowledged each of the directions then knelt and placed her palm on the ground. "Mother Earth."

She closed her eyes and breathed in a deep slow breath and released it, stood and reached her hand to the skies.

"Father Sun, Grandmother Moon, to the Star Nations." She closed her eyes, breathed deep, opened her eyes and smiled. Tranquility washed through Justine, and the fatigue from her physical labor subsided. Energy and excitement burst in her stomach.

"It's time to meet Thy Shadow Self." Grandmother's dark brown eyes burrowed into Justine's soul.

Justine's chest thrust out as she choked on a gasp.

"Come." The old woman stood. They followed her into the darkened forest. Cold swept across Justine's skin, leaving a path of goose bumps.

"There." The old women pointed to a shadow now taking on a creepy human form sitting on a rock. "You must capture it."

The inside of Justine's chest froze. Her body quivered and lip trembled. "Why? How?"

"The same way one would capture a wild animal."

"But I wouldn't capture a wild animal."

The old woman stared at Justine. "Chase it until it's exhausted. When you grab onto it, don't let go—no matter what."

"Shane?"

He stepped toward her. His grandmother clutched his arm and tugged him back.

"She must do this alone."

SHADOW SELF

Justine sucked in a deep breath past the fear solidifying in her chest and crept toward the shadow. Each step on the mossy forest floor released the damp scent of mushrooms. The shadow leapt from the rock and bolted between trees. She rushed after it. Over rocks, under logs, across creeks. Branches scratched bare arms and legs, leaving streaks of blood as she thrashed through the forest after the eerie form that traveled with ease through the dense woods. Sweat soaked her T-shirt. Her body quivered as it weakened. The shadow stumbled over a root and fell to the ground. Her legs trembled and heart battered her chest walls as she dove on top of the jelled figure. It flattened like mush under her and then swelled to a more solid rubbery substance. It twisted and turned and flipped her off. She reached out and clutched it by the arm. Her fingers sank deep inside the slippery body. A nonhuman squeal resonated in the air. The shape kicked, clawed, punched, and slapped. The brutal lashes stung her skin.

Don't let go no matter what. She pressed it tight to the ground until it lost its fight.

"Bring it back to the sacred circle." Grandmother waved.

Justine dragged the exhausted villain toward the clearing with the rock formation. Bursts of rage sent the shadow into a kicking and screaming frenzy.

Don't let go no matter what. Justine clenched and fought her own fatigue, pulling and dragging the creature into the clearing before throwing it inside the circle. As soon as it landed on the blessed ground, it manifested into pliable flesh and bones, a sickly replica of a human. Scrawny hands attempted to conceal its tiny breast and crotch. Swollen eyes, surrounded by black and set deep in its skull, glared at Justine. Gusts of wind erupted and tossed its tangled hair. Gaunt shoulders, backbone and rib cage protruded through a thin layer of skin as it coiled into a fetal position, shivering. Slight squeaks and moans escaped its thin lips.

Fear thrashed through Justine. Pity for the creature consumed her as she stepped into the circle peeling her T-shirt off. Goose bumps popped across her bare flesh. Confusion swirled in her head. It peered out from under a skeletal arm and snarled. Justine froze then forced another step.

With eyes flaring red, it bolted up. Slobber drooled from its toothless mouth as it screeched. Fear held Justine's feet to the ground. She stared back at Shane who stood wideeyed with his arms wrapped around his grandmother. He stepped toward the circle. Grandmother tugged him back.

Small steps took Justine closer to the being. It watched from under its arm. Justine reached the T-shirt toward her. The creature sat up as Justine walked forward, placed the T-shirt over its head and pulled its arms through the holes.

The creature stretched the shirt to the ground and under its feet. Hugging its knees, rocking.

Justine mirrored its position but held steady. "What are you?" Justine's muscles tensed.

"You."

"Excuse me?" Anger pulsated through Justine.

"I am you. All that you have repressed, left undeveloped, denied. All that is unconscious in you." It thrust itself forward and screeched. "How could you make me like this? How? How could you leave me alone to fend for myself?"

Fear rushed through Justine's body. "I…I didn't even know you existed."

"Liar! Denial is not the same as not knowing! Liar!" It lunched. Wretched breath scorched Justine's face.

"I-I… didn't…" A huge lump itched her throat. Tears blurred her vision and guilt churned in her stomach.

"Liar! Liaaaaarrr! Liaaaaaaarrrrrr! Liaaaaaaaarrrrr!" Red eyes flared. Foam drooled from its twisted lips.

Justine retreated and fell backward onto her hands. Anger boiled inside her. She bolted, stood and towered over the shaking creature.

"Okay, it's true! It's because you repulse me! You are weak and pathetic! You let people use and abuse you. I hate you! I hate you! I hate you!"

"I am you!"

"Stop saying that!"

"I am you! I am you! I am you! I am you!"

Justine pushed herself toward the creature, clutched its skeletal shoulders, and shook hard. "Stop it!"

The creature stilled at her touch. Tears swelled in her dark vacant eyes. A voice barely audible squeaked out, "You left me alone to face the shadows."

Guilt and remorse filled Justine as she looked at the dismal, gaunt replica of herself. "I'm sorry." Her voice not much louder. Justine pulled the creature close and wrapped her arms tight around her.

The two melded into one as the vision of Justine's life unfolded at rapid speed in her mind. Memories of Karmas in her childhood dreams played out like a movie. They'd frolicked for hours in streams and fields filled with flowers. She rode his back up steep mountains and clung to him as he swam across lakes. She curled into his softness under moonlit skies, knowing she was safe and sleep would take her away. He traveled with her in the wakened state although unseen to the naked eye in her daily life. She saw the world as a secure place and had no doubt this magnificent protector at her side made her invincible. Before her teen years, life proved her wrong.

Anger rose, remembering how Karmas disappeared when she needed him the most. Puke rushed to her throat, recalling how she had screamed for Karmas.

Eleven years old, the first time she had stayed out past dark and so thankful that she had Karmas at her side as she hurried past the alley toward home. From behind a calloused palm smothered her lips and nose. Her feet flipped out from under her as he hauled her with heels skidding and flesh peeling against the pavement, behind a dumpster. Strong groping hands of a stranger pushed her to the wall, pressed his sweat-drenched body against hers and breathed hot whiskey breath into her mouth, slobbering on her with his tongue. Coarse whiskers scratched her face as she struggled to free herself. She knew that Karmas would come and pull this wretched beast from her, rip him to shreds and leave him in the alley to die. But instead, she lay in the alley wishing to die, half nude with slime all over her. Karmas now nothing more than a figment of her imagination. She gathered her clothes under the starless sky and staggered around the corner to her home, numb lips quivering like the rest of her body.

Her mother's vacant gaze. "Why didn't you come home when you were told? When are you going to listen? Damn you, child! Maybe now you'll learn!" Her father's scowl of disgust and dead silence. The doctor cleaning her up with much less compassion than the vet had bestowed on her cat that had a piece of glass in its foot. The officer demanding she stop behaving like a spoiled child and answer his questions. The judgmental stares from the rest of the world— the stares.

The night she disobeyed and broke curfew—never mentioned again—in words.

Bitterness triumphed over her shame and she pushed the bear from her life once and for all. She acknowledged fantasies and dreams were just that and delved into school studies and dealt only with reality—someone else's idea of reality. She saw herself separating into two and moving away from the weakest part, her Shadow Self. She watched herself pouring all of her hate, revulsion, disgust, shame, and loneliness into her Shadow Self, forcing it away. Pushing, loathing, and blaming it more with each disappointment life dealt her.

Justine stopped and stared at the familiar soul hovering above the shadow reaching out, projecting its warmth. She went back over the visions. That soul had been there all along, attempting to get close. Each time her Shadow Self batted it away like an irritating fly. Justine gasped as she recognized it as Shane's soul.

"I love you." She heard herself saying.

The world shifted from grays to vibrant colors.

Justine opened her eyes and clung to Shane, sobbing.

"Shane." Her throat hurt.

"Shhhh, it's okay, Justine, just cry."

She shook as she sobbed in his arms. He held her.

Her cries subsided. She breathed deep and pulled away, embarrassed. "Shane?"

He stroked her hair.

"Shane…thank you."

He ran his palms down her arms and squeezed her hands. "You're welcome."

She focused on his eyes.

"Shane, you…your soul was there throughout the whole thing. My whole life."

He returned her stare. "I know." He swallowed. "It appears that I've always loved you." Her eyes widened.

"And I think in more than just this lifetime."

"Shane…"

"He shrugged and looked down. "It's okay, Justine, you don't have to say anything."

"Yes, I do. I love you too, Shane." His bright eyes held hers.

"How can you be sure you're not just reeling from that experience?"

"Because I know I loved you before we even came out here."

"Really?" His eyes widened.

"Really."

"I've always loved you, Justine, always. Even when it was wrong to love you. I couldn't help it. I love you."

"I have always loved you too."

He jumped to his feet, thrust his face toward the moon, and shouted, "She loves me! I can't believe she loves me!" Wolves howled.

She wanted to laugh, but the disturbance in her body still ruled.

Twigs snapped behind them. They turned to see a huge brown bear plodding into their camp.

Justine stepped toward it. "Karmas!"

Shane clutched her arm and yanked her back.

"Justine, no!"

She pulled herself free from his grip. "Shane, it's Karmas, I'm sure it is!"

The bear froze and stared at them.

Shane gripped her arm. "Even if it is, he's a wild animal in this world."

The bear turned and ran into the forest.

Shane pulled her into his arms. "I have waited a lifetime to do this." He touched his lips to hers. She parted her lips and played her tongue inside his mouth. He pressed his mouth against hers.

Warmth swam to her soul. Fatigue swept over her. She pulled away. "Shane, I'm sorry. I need sleep."

"Let's go to bed."

They crawled into the tent and scuttled into their sleeping bags. Shane pulled Justine close and held her as she sobbed throughout the night, reliving in detail each vision she had with her Shadow Self.

Smothering heat woke Justine. She opened her eyes and looked at Shane's empty sleeping bag. She sat up, kneeled in front of the door, unzipped it and poked her head through the opening. "Is it safe to come out?"

"Hi, beautiful." Shane chuckled. "Who knows what safe is anymore."

She crawled out and stood. "I have never felt safer." She walked over and wrapped her arms around him. Aroma of greasy bacon, eggs and strong coffee filled the air.

"Are you okay?"

"I am. Thank you." She cuddled into him.

He held her at arm's length. "Do you still love me or was that just last night?" His voice teased, but his eyes pleaded.

"I love you, Shane. I can't get over how much I love you." She placed her hand on the small of his back and yanked him close. His hardness pressed against her.

"I've been trying real hard, but I can't wait another minute." His breath hot in her ear. "I need you now."

She tugged away. "Inside the tent."

He lifted the pan off the camp stove, shut it off and followed close behind her. Fever rushed her quivering body as he fumbled with the buttons on her top and slid it over her shoulders. Muscles on his back molded into her palms as she glided her hands under his shirt and lifted it over his head. Tingles of lust swept down her body at the touch of his warm fingers brushing against her stomach, while he slipped them inside the waistband of her jeans, and struggled to undo the snap. Tenderly, she pushed his hands aside, undid the snap with ease, wiggled her jeans to the floor and stepped out of them.

The sudden awareness that she was nude in front of him stirred an embarrassment and she glanced away. With pants hugging his ankles, he bounced on one foot trying to get the pant leg over his heel, and tumbled on the bed. A flush of red moved up his face. She stifled her giggles, unlaced and removed his shoes, then tugged off his pants. Gentle arms pulled her on top of him. Warmth from their bare skin touching swept over her, and all awkwardness vanished with the surging passion.

Vibrations of his deep moans tickled her lips as she softly teased the flesh of his neck. She breathed in the scent of the woodsy cologne that she had craved for so long. His body trembled under her roaming kisses. Shivers owned her flesh as his soft mouth and tongue explored her curves, leaving a path of swelling desire. Their feverish bodies melded and pulsated as one, inventing a rhythm new to the universe until their passion exploded in unison and lay exhausted.

"Oh my god, I never knew it could be like that." Her heart still pounded.

He opened his mouth, but no words came out.

She giggled, curled up next to him and fell asleep.

Justine rolled over and stretched. Beads of perspiration slid down her nude body. This tent is like an oven. She looked over at Shane sleeping. Sweat glistening off his muscular shoulders. She reached down and massaged him awake. He moaned, opened his eyes, and smiled. She slithered over onto his heated flesh and sucked on his salty neck as their bodies and souls united in a frenzy of passion.

The Ceremony

Justine woke to Shane staring at her. He bent over and kissed her lips.

"I need to go say good-bye to my grandmother."

"Okay."

"Come with me?"

"Of course."

They pulled on their clothes and crawled out of the tent.

Shane flipped a blanket on the ground. "I think we'll be more comfortable here. Are you ready?" Justine nodded.

They lay on the blanket, clinging to each other. Warmth surged through her as their foreheads touched. Light purple filled her vision and surrounded them.

Grandmother sat on a log. "We need a labyrinth."

Shane looked at Justine and grinned. "That means us."

"Is that like a maze?"

Grandmother nodded. "Yes, but with only one path in and the same path out."

Justine and Shane hauled rocks and placed them in a huge spiral creating a path to the center.

She whispered in his ear, "I'm scared to ask what this is for."

He forced a chuckle. "Me too." He placed the last rock in the large space in center.

Justine plopped on the ground and wiped her damp forehead with her shirtsleeve.

The old woman pointed to a flock of swans descending with the setting sun. "Go now to the lake and bathe with mud and water." Justine leaned toward Shane and whispered, "Wash with mud?"

He shrugged, took her hand in his and they walked to the end of the path. Water gushed from the top of a mountain between flourishing green plants and splashed into a dark pool surrounded by lush foliage and shimmering in the red and yellow sunset. Slender white necks reflected from the water.

He pulled Justine close and held her face in his hands. "I love you, Justine. I want to spend my life with you."

"I love you too, Shane. This is forever."

Deep drumming filled the air. They looked up to where they left Grandmother. Déjà vu consumed her. She watched as Shane stripped nude, did the same and dashed into the water. The swans scattered into the iridescent sky. Shane and Justine dove to the bottom of the warm pool and scooped handfuls of black mud, surfaced, crawled onto shore and smeared the mud over each other's body and scrubbed it into their hair. Covered with sludge, they plunged into the pool. She tilted her head back into the water and combed her fingers through her hair. They scooped water up and rubbed their palms and fingertips over one another until all traces of muck were gone. Just as the moon pulled itself high in the sky, they crawled out of the lagoon into the hot air. Moonlight shimmered off a red silky robe draped over a large rock.

"Is this for me?" Justine lifted the long gown.

He shrugged. "I suspect so."

She slipped her head into the opening, dropped it over her nude body, and flipped the hood over her damp hair.

He picked up a matching robe and stepped into it. "You look beautiful." He pulled his hood over his head.

She smiled. "As do you."

"What do you think this is about?"

"Some sort of ceremony we are to partake in?"

In unison, their heads spun toward the clearing, as a pounding of drums intensified. She slid her hand into his and the two walked up the hill toward the rhythm. A glow shone at the top of the hill.

They rounded the corner to see that flickering candles lined the labyrinth. Grandmother and Kitchamia sat in the center, slapping the skins of their drums. Both in long white robes with hoods trimmed in red. Pine gum smouldered from the red coal, set in a small circle of rocks. A white leather book sat next to it. Grandmother stood and stretched her arms out to them. They hesitated, looked at each other, stepped into the labyrinth and followed the spiral one small step after another.

Grandmother scooped the book, flipped it open, revealing large gold typescript and balanced it in her palms. Flames from the candles flickered off a red satin ribbon that draped through the spine of the book and hung from both sides tickling the ground.

"I feel like we're at our wedding." Justine looked at Shane.

"I think we might be," he whispered back.

Kitchamia turned to the north and thrust his hand into the air. Grandmother pulled her book close to her chest and imitated Kitchamia.

"From the winds of the North." "From the winds of the South." "From the winds of the West."

"From the winds of the East."

Gandmother and Kithamia knelt and placed their palms on the ground.

"Mother Earth."

They stood and reached for the sky.

"Father Sun, Grandmother Moon, Stars."

Kitchamia stepped next to Grandmother. Shane and Justine faced the two, gripping each other's sweaty palms.

Grandmother spoke in a clear concise voice, "Children of the earth, we are gathered here again under the command of fire, water, earth and air."

Justine's and Shane's faces swung toward each other's. "Again?" they said in unison.

They looked deep into one another's pupils and watched a vision unfold of the two of them standing in front of this very altar in another lifetime.

"Justine and Shane, the choice is yours. Will you bind your love for a year and a day, a lifetime, or for all of eternity?" Grandmother waited for them to speak.

In the vision swirling in each other's eyes, they saw themselves answering "a year and a day." The vision flipped to a new ceremony where they answered "a lifetime."

Justine gasped. "This is our wedding."

Shane returned her stare. The stunned look matched his stammering voice. "Justine, I swear, I didn't know—"
"For all of eternity!" Justine smiled.

"Really? You want to go through with this?"

"Yes. I do." Fear rushed Justine. She moved back. "Why, don't you?"

"I do, for all of eternity!"

Kitchamia stepped forward, lifted each of their hands, and layered their wrists. He pulled the long ribbon from the book and draped it over their arms. He slid the soft satin over their skin and swathed it around and in between their hands and wrists. Shane stared into Justin's eyes as Kitchamia tugged the binding snug and bound it in a knot. Tears of relief slid down Justine's face as the familiar tight ribbon bound her to the soul she loved once again.

Kitchamia spoke, "With this rope, we fasten your love for all of eternity and bless you with warmth from fire, freshness of water, depths of earth and pureness of air." Justine and Shane faced one another.

Justine breathed deep. "I love you, all of who you were, who you are and who you will become, with all that I was, all that I am and all that I will become. I will walk with you along the path of life and cherish you always." Moisture blurred her vision as she watched Shane's eyes pooling with tears.

"Justine, I have waited multiple lifetimes for this moment. All that I am is yours. Now and forever and into eternity from this lifetime to the next. I love you with all my heart, body and soul."

Kitchamia unwound the ribbon and draped it around the back of Grandmother's neck. She nodded at Kitchamia, smiled then focused on the couple.

"And now, by the power of fire, water, earth and air, the blessings of Mother Earth, Father Sun, Grandmother Moon and the Stars, I give you each other for all of eternity." They leaned forward until Shane's soft warm lips touched Justine's.

A New Reality

They opened their eyes and stared at one another. They sat up and looked over at the tent. The long red ribbon wrapped around a pole and flapped in the wind.

The moon burst from behind a cloud, cascading a beam of light on them. An owl overhead hooted. A wolf howled then another and another until the night air filled with nature's finest symphony.

Shane looked in the direction of the howls. "I do believe they're playing our song." He reached his hand toward her. "May I have this dance?"

They clung to each other. Their bodies moving in time to the earth's rhythm. Justine lingered between laughing and crying. She did both.

"Ready to call it a night?" Shane asked.

"Uh-huh."

Shane spread the smouldering coals with a long piece of wood, and they crawled into the tent with the flashlight shining. Justine unzipped her sleeping bag and laid it flat. Shane did the same, placing his over top. They stripped nude and slid between the covers. The light from the flashlight disappeared. The glow of the moon saturated the inside of the dome. Their naked skin slid together as they consummated their marriage in harmony with the howling wolves.

Justine poked her head out of the tent and grinned. "Are you going to make me breakfast every morning for the rest of my life?"

A smile spread across his face as he flipped an egg. "If you want me to."

"I do." She crawled out and stretched nude under the hot sun.

"If you promise to come to breakfast every morning wearing that, I promise to make the breakfast."

"Deal." She walked over and wrapped her arms around him. He lifted the pan off the flames and set it to the side, lifted her into his arms and carried her to the blanket spread across the ground. "But, of course, breakfast will have to wait."

"Of course."

A flock of birds landed on the trees close by and serenaded the morning as Justine and Shane's worlds merged.

The birds rose with a clatter and disappeared. He rolled over and caressed her mouth with his soft fingertips.

"I love you, Wife."

"I love you too, Husband."

She smiled and stood. "Let's go wash up."

They strolled to the stream arm in arm. She dipped her toe in and shivered. Goose bumps covered her entire body. She jumped in and shrieked, reached to the bottom and pulled up a handful of mud, and stood and stepped onto the ground. She smoothed the mud over her skin and through her hair. Returned to the stream and sat in it. Shane waded in, gasped, and splashed water over himself. He reached for a handful of mud and smeared it over his body. She tilted her head back into the water and combed the mud out with her fingers.

They stepped out. She held her arms out and chuckled.

"No red robe waiting?"

The slight breeze dried their bodies as they walked shivering and nude back to the tent and pulled on clean clothes. Across from the hot fire, they ate their cold eggs and bacon.

He broke the silence. "How do we go back to practicing psychiatry after this?"

"Not so sure we do."

"But it's our life."

"So we adjust our style of therapy."

"Do you think people are ready for this?"

She laughed loud. "No."

"We might be surprised. I sure wouldn't have thought I was ready for this."

She nodded. "Me neither." She stared at nothing. "I don't even know how we could go back to the city after this."

"So let's pick another place to live." He jumped to his feet, rushed to his truck and returned flipping open a map.

"Let's ask our guides to take us to a spiritual place."

"We can open our own practice."

They unfolded the map like children opening Christmas gifts, laid it across the ground and knelt over it.

He crawled behind her, pressed his body against hers and covered her eyes with his palms. "Point to our new home."

Justine extended her index finger and dropped it onto the map.

"Looks like we are going to Canada, Crowsnest Pass in Southern Alberta." He grinned. "Wherever that is."